BROWN BREAD IN WENGEN

Nicky Burkett wasn't expecting a dead MP on his doorstep. Nor was he planning on the world and his wife having something to say about it. Next thing he knows, Nicky's got to take the heat from the Old Bill and every Tom, Dick and Harry; and his missus ain't happy, either. Nicky is supposed to be keeping clean — he can't afford not to. But the dirty trail of revenge on the posh slopes of Wengen, combined with Mickey Cousins' lot and their penchant for aggro, make it pretty hard to resist being drawn into the fray . . .

Books by Jeremy Cameron
Published by Ulverscroft:

VINNIE GOT BLOWN AWAY
IT WAS AN ACCIDENT

JEREMY CAMERON

BROWN BREAD
IN WENGEN

Complete and Unabridged

ULVERSCROFT
Leicester

First published in Great Britain in 2015 by
HopeRoad Publishing Ltd
London

First Large Print Edition
published 2017
by arrangement with
HopeRoad Publishing Ltd
London

A catalogue record for this book is available
from the British Library.

ISBN 978–1–4448–3153–5

Published by
F. A. Thorpe (Publishing)
Anstey, Leicestershire

Set by Words & Graphics Ltd.
Anstey, Leicestershire
Printed and bound in Great Britain by
T. J. International Ltd., Padstow, Cornwall

This book is printed on acid-free paper

1

Dead geezer was waiting on my stairs.

'Evening geezer,' I went.

He never answered.

There I was, got the tea to cook. Needed to get out and buy an eighth off Jimmy Foley before Noreen came home. Fucking dead geezer reckoned he'd be waiting for me. It was inconsiderate.

I kicked him. He still never answered.

Wasn't used to clocking dead geezers. Excepting the two I wasted by accident I never clocked anyone who got the big one.

Never ought to get past the outside door only the fucking people downstairs kept on losing their keys so they left the Chubb off and came in the Yale with their cash card. Same way the geezer did probably.

'Jesus,' I turned round and said. 'As if I ain't got troubles enough.'

Went in our door and put the groceries down. Switched the kettle on and checked the time. Five o'clock. George my warrant officer ought to be home by now. I belled him. 'George mate,' I turned round and said.

'Oh my good Gawd,' he went.

'Good to chat to you George,' I goes. 'Always good to check you out you knows that.'

'Nicky,' he goes, 'can't you ring the bleeding office like anyone else does? How did you get my home number when I just changed it again? S'pose you're bringing me nothing but grief?'

'Grief never comes handy George,' I goes philosophical. 'Grief waits for no geezer. What it is George see, I comes home minding no one's business except my own and what do I find? Only a dead geezer. Dead geezer croaked on my stairs is all.'

'Dead geezer? You got a dead geezer on your stairs?'

'I believe that's what I just turned round and said George.'

'Jesus Nicky it follows you around, don't it? You kill him?'

'Fuck's sake George! Told you he was sat here waiting! Waiting dead.'

'You know who he is?'

'I ain't got no fuckin' idea. Definitely a geezer. Ain't no bird. Cuts it down.'

'You sure he's dead? You tested his pulse?'

'No George I ain't tested his pulse. I ain't given him no mouth-to-mouth job neither.'

'Nicky you test his pulse then you ring the hospital straight away, you get me? Tell them

2

if he's alive or dead before they start out.'

'No George I ain't doing that.'

'Why not Nicky for God's sake?'

'Well George there ain't generally no call for checking a geezer's pulse when he got the back of his bonce smashed up and then, just in case you got any doubt, it looks like they strangled him in the bargain, being as how he got his tongue down his chin and he got a rope round his neck.'

'Jesus.'

'Then they shot him in the back George, part of the package.'

'God Nicky.'

'They never liked him George.'

'It don't sound like it.'

'They never wanted him borrowing no more fivers till giro day.'

'Nicky you got to get on the blower right off. 999, police, ambulance, the lot.'

'Fire brigade?'

'No never mind the fire brigade only you ring the police now — '

'George I got you for my warrant officer so I rings you when I got a problem. You knows how they mess with you when you got a bit of form. Never fancy getting a kicking round them cells just on account of some geezer got brown bread on my stairs. Want you there George please mate like a witness you reckon seeing as how you're Old Bill. Look after my interests like.'

'Jesus Nicky, you ain't heard they privatised us? I ain't in the bleeding police force any more, I'm a bleeding civilian. They gave me the choice Nicky, be a civilian or go back on the beat. You ain't heard?'

Heard all right. George gave me the news about a million times over. One unhappy geezer. Made my heart bleed.

'Yeah George only once Old Bill always Old Bill innit? Maybe no one told them up Chingford anyway.'

'And Nicky you reckon I'm your warrant officer but you're forgetting you're straight these days, ain't that right? No more fines? Only thing you did the last couple of years was kill someone and they never did fine people for that.'

'It was an accident George and anyway you may have forgot the stress and tribulation on me like my brief turned round and said. Like I never will recover from that stress. Truth George they ought to give me compensation dosh for all that, not start the other way round innit?'

George he made a rude noise.

'Knew you'd help me out George, so I sit here and wait while you come round with Old Bill.'

'Jesus Nicky . . . '

So I cut him then belled Noreen, got her just before she left work, told her go by her mum till I checked her there. Gave her the bones, give her the rest later. Told her it was never down to me some geezer came round dead.

Noreen sounded like she never gave it much cred. Even you told the truth your woman never believed it. Fact was she sounded upset. Get on my case about dead geezers coming round her place. Maybe give her a spot of emotion later bring her round. Bit of sobbing always helped with birds.

★ ★ ★

I took a close-up on the back of his bonce.

Bits oozing out. You reckon inside some geezer's Judge Dread they got to have a load of gravy. Not this geezer's. White bits, brown bits, black bits all mash up. Like pebble dash and my mum's rice pudding mixed together, melt him down for bonemeal and put him on your garden. Only a bit of hot sauce lying on top.

One other point you got to mention before Old Bill came round. He was wearing a suit. And shiny shoes. So he never came up Howard Road brassick. And like as not he was carrying pennies. I put on Noreen's gardening gloves. Four pot plants and she bought state-of-the-fucking-monte gardening gloves. I lifted his wallet. Never checked his cards or his bleeding family photos or whatnot. Only borrowed a century. Left another two still there. No problem.

Arrangement with Noreen was I never went out committing crimes or I was history. Not the case I reckoned I never committed crimes that came by my door. Not even a crime you looked at it sensible. Feller never had the need any more. Wanted me to have it.

His neck was a state you had to reckon. Rope near as took his head off. Eyes popping. True as I stood here his tongue hung down his chin. Gravy came out his hooter and his lugs. Then more off his back where they plugged him. All over the fucking stairs and who cleaned it up? I got permanent aggravation off downstairs about who cleaned the fucking staircase. Landlord never wanted to know. I reckoned it got to be their responsibility downstairs. Fair enough I used the stairs for climbing up only they got them all day.

Geezer was smelling already. Maybe he smelled like that before he signed off. I went and brewed the tea.

Fucking hundreds of them and not one gave me any more cred than Noreen. Nor went for that emotion.

Old Bill never believed anyone, principle, only they extra never believed me. All on account of how I had a bit of bother way back with a chief superintendent.

They sat down in my gaff never asked.

'Look fellers,' I went. 'Look fellers you all know me right, know how I was always helpful?'

Reckoned I heard some fucker spit somewhere.

'You got DSTT Holdsworth on duty?'

'TT's on a course,' they went. 'Interpersonal skills.'

Then we all burst out cackling and it got a bit easier after that so I got the rum out. They still never believed me only they never arrested you after you got the rum out, count on it.

'You know who he is?' went that CID Inspector, name of Forrest. 'This dead geezer on your stairs?'

'He ain't a well man, all I know. And he don't smell too healthy. He one of yours?'

'MP for Chingford is all. You got a dead Member of Parliament on your door Nicky.

What you make of that then?'

'Heard they was always the best ones dead ones.'

'Oliver Mannion.'

'Never clocked him. What the fuck he come round here for?'

'That's what we were hoping you could tell us. You got a dead fucking MP!'

'Do me a favour geezer. I ain't got no fuckin' notion.'

'Make you right on that one,' goes some nasty little fucker, DC something, Gillespie. 'Bet you never even heard of your own MP, leave alone Chingford.'

'Get your notes out you want to bet,' I goes.

'Pardon?'

'You reckon you want to bet, get your paper out.'

He went a bit pale only he never could reverse now. Put on his smug look instead, reckoned he'd call me and boost his rep. 'How much?' he goes. All the rest got interested now, even the scene-of-crime geezers stopped their dusting and wiping and pulled round.

'Score.'

'Er . . . '

'Put it out.'

He got his wallet and they all checked him

shuffling. Put a twenty on the table and I matched it. Old Bill never believed their little mince pies now.

'Alan Carmody,' I goes.

'Shit.'

'Had a pint with him Saturday down the Pig and Whistle.' I picked up the dosh.

'You fucking little bastard.'

'Come in handy a bit extra, ring my dealer later purchase some of that illegal cannabis. Giro never did go far enough.'

They had to hold him back. They all cackled in the bargain. 'Lucky he don't arrest you,' goes one of them. 'Just going off shift is Gillespie, likes to make a nicking just before he finishes so he has to stay on for the paperwork, three hours' overtime.' Then one of them stood there, big blonde bird name of Burns, and would you believe when she finished clocking me up and down she pulled out her visiting card and put it on the table. Big tits in the bargain. Problem I had with uniformed birds, always got this problem wondered what it was like their buttons got undone. No doubting she fancied it.

'And I never want you fitting me up neither on some piece of shit,' I turned round and said that Gillespie.

'Lot of witnesses here, George you be my

witness innit? Malicious arrest he comes after me?'

'Hrmph,' goes George.

'Little fucker,' goes DC Gillespie.

'You fellers finished now you drunk all the rum?' I went. 'Or you want to start on that cannabis? I got some good skunk I put somewhere, you seen it any place?'

They all went home after that. Took their MP with them, experts finished sorting him out. You got to turn round and say pigs were strange geezers. One way they reckoned whacking your MP was crime of the century. Other way they reckoned it was a fucking good laugh.

And I belled Noreen told her come home.

* * *

'Got them Laura Ashley pies for your tea Noreen,' I turned round and said. 'Bit pricey only I knows you likes them.'

'Linda McCartney Nicky not Laura Ashley. Stop winding me up. Only I got my tea round Mum's. Put it in the freezer eh? I brought you some of my mum's gravy, go with your pie if you want.'

'Your mum's a little darling. Just like you course Noreen.'

'Won't get round me like that Nicky, best

10

tell me what's been going down. You know I warned you Nicky, more of them crimes and we're finished you and me, you know that.'

'Noreen be fair! You ain't even heard the knockings yet!'

I was half cut after that boozing with the filth. Getting the sleepy stage, all I wanted was a little sit down and maybe a feel up my bird. Only Noreen was never even getting started. She was sniffing me up suspicious like I was a criminal type.

'Do me a favour Noreen know what I mean?'

When she got mean that Noreen she got a nasty habit closing her little beadies up. Eyelash job. Make a geezer para just sitting there. When she sucked her teeth the same time you got big problems.

'Noreen I only went out bought them Laura Ashley pies . . . '

She whacked me.

'Linda McCartney pies and special for you a bit of that Michael Jackson muesli and Whitney Houston pattie and dumplings . . . ' She started giggling. 'And Marley's Black Forest Gateau and that Diana Ross chocolate pudding and chocolate sauce . . . '

She jumped me on the settee, banged her little fists on my bonce and I felt her tits scrunching all round on me never failed on getting me going. She moved a leg up. Now was time for getting the words in before she turned nasty again.

'Noreen straight up I never reckoned the geezer. Fuck knows what he was after. Could be he was a tief man come to roust us.'

'Oh yeah Chingford MP after your giro money I suppose.'

'Maybe he heard you got a personal computer Noreen.'

'Yeah, never afford one himself, blah-di-blah.'

'Maybe he got lost. Maybe he got that memory loss or he was after a bit of stuff, heard that Shelley Rosario got a gaff round the corner.'

'And speaking of bits of stuff Nicky — '

'Eh?'

'Speaking of bits of stuff — '

'Who was speaking of bits of stuff?'

'When I came in the door I smelled woman.'

'What!'

'Woman smell, what I smelled. Woman smell. Who been coming up here then Nicky, eh?'

'Jesus Noreen, which you rather, I killed someone or I had a bit of bird up here?'

'Answer the question Nicky.' She gave me that very nasty eyes-closed-teeth-suck.

I never helped it. 'Jesus Noreen,' I turned round and said, 'maybe you want to bell Chingford nick ask what you smelled. One of them Old Bill was a bird. Big blonde bird name of Burns. Bit tits. I never smelled her close up never do that with pigs, only you got a better nose than me no problem Noreen . . . ' Her little mince pies were opening up. 'Right little raver that PC Burns, took me down the alley after and you never credit how she moved, and teeth — telling you I got love bites all over — '

She whacked me more and giggled and undid my shirt looking for love bites only then she started kissing me and giving little licks, she knew how she drove me careless that Noreen. Body like a fucking angel and little muscles straight out the gym, best bit of woman in Walthamstow. Got a brain too or so she kept telling me. Drive any geezer careless . . .

'Only just you remember Nicky . . . '

'Remember what Noreen? Remember your birthday? Remember buy the toilet paper?'

'Remember you stray out of line and I cut it off man. Just one little sniff is all it takes.'

'One little sniff? You gonna cut off my hooter Noreen?'

'Not unless your hooter's what you put up them women Nicky. You do that? You like to put your hooter up your women?' She was starting up snorting with laughing, her own hooter job here.

'Be surprised what some birds like Noreen. Specially Old Bill women so I heard, WPCs lot of them fancy a real good nose up . . . '

She was rolling all over me now cackling like a donkey. 'Well you just keep your little nose jobs for them others,' she goes. 'For me though, you can reserve your nice bit of elastic down there Nicky, do the trick just nicely.'

'What you say lady.'

'Now why you think that Chingford MP was coming round your flat?'

'Fuck knows. You want to come to bed?'

'All right. Don't mind if I do.'

Never could tell with birds. Twelve months telling me how I was staying off crime. Then crime came sitting on my doorstep and she only got leery on some WPC. Never could tell.

2

Morning came Noreen went off for working. She got a Class A number down British Airways their office up the West End. On account of she passed exams at school, did computers and talked polite like. And on account of how she looked like about four million dollars. So she got a number up west. Left home 8.20 in the morning, got there 8.55 squeezed in the rush hour. Anyone finger her in the tube and I shaft them.

When I came out of nick all my mates got together and touched me that flat. Mates and our Sharon. Paid the deposit and first few weeks. First gaff I ever got on my own. Lived one time up that Kelly when we got the kid only never got a place my own. Just before I got released Kelly started fucking a German. By that time though my mates and our Sharon got me the gaff so it never mattered. The kid Danny came down visiting.

Noreen started in the bargain. Then some fucker gave her one long thin dark scar on my account, her ear down her throat. Never make it up to her. Still she kept coming visiting. Most brilliant bit of woman in town and I got her.

Then she reckoned she was moving in. Not a case of arguing.

Noreen went off to work and I got up Chingford CID answer more of their questions.

Only before I got there it was all over the fucking papers.

Fucking Alexander kept ringing only I never answered it. Never had an answermachine either, never wanted to hear their fucking messages. Mobile was another matter, strictly personal. I answered it.

It was that Bridget Tansley off the *Walthamstow Guardian*. Young bird training up.

'Nicky,' she turned round and said.

'Bridget. How's them courts and Council meetings?'

'Nicky you're in the news do you know that? Everyone's trying to get you, they'll be round your address soon. This is the biggest story in Walthamstow for years. Do you want to give me an exclusive?'

Plenty of things I wanted to give her only not an exclusive. 'No Bridget I never want to give you an exclusive.'

'Not even when we worked so well before? Nicky, an MP was murdered round your flat.

People are checking you out. They've all heard that this sort of thing . . . has happened to you before. Do you want to give me a break here so I can protect your interests?'

'Bollocks Bridget you know that.'

'Yeah I know that Nicky, sorry but they tell us to say that sort of thing. Being straight with you, you want to tell me what he was doing round your flat?'

'You find out Bridget, you let me know, eh? Fucked if I know, I never even clapped my little porkies on him before. No problem Bridget no hard feelings only I just can't yack to you, know what I mean?'

I went unobtainable. I was getting stitched up here.

All I wanted was collect my giro once a fortnight and feel up my bird. Buy a bit of draw and get pissed up down the boozer Saturdays. Not part of the plan finding geezers croaked on my door, not part of the plan at all.

I went out and belled Mrs Mellow my brief from a callbox. Wanted her up Chingford nick answer the questions on my account. Most briefs never be arsed coming up the nick when there was never any wedge in it, only Mrs Mellow never gave any geezer the knock back. Trouble was she was up court now.

No one else I could take got any cred.

17

Andy my old probation not such a bad geezer, only I heard he was down the fucking Channel tunnel same as usual. George my warrant, get a seizure you asked him be a witness so his mates don't give you a kicking round the cells. Not very wise asking Bridget off the paper, interview be on CNN in four minutes. I cabbed it up fucking Chingford on my tod. Bit of a problem being a murder witness. Fucking sight simpler do the business yourself.

★ ★ ★

Just when I went in the front door they were letting Dean Longmore out. Dean supposed to be straight these days so he reckoned, only it was like the bananas they wanted up the supermarkets for that Common Market. No matter how you wanted the fucking banana straight, never the way it was meant to be.

'Dean,' I goes in the doorway.

'Nicky what you in for? They only after stitching me on a Receiving, credit that?'

'Yeah I credit that Dean. Probably that load of jackets you had last week innit?'

'Nicky shut the fuck up, you hear what I'm saying? Feller got to do a bit of work.'

'Yeah Dean.'

'You knows how I'm straight Nicky these

18

days, makes my dosh fetching them motors back off the Costa Geriatrica.'

'And Receiving.'

'I'm a businessman Nicky. Anyway what you doing here, dropped in for a cup of rosie or what?'

'Help the fucking Old Bill with their fucking inquiries Dean.'

'Oh yeah you got problems I heard.'

'Fucking Chingford MP got problems, finished up relaxing on my stairs last night. No pulse.'

'Jesus Nicky you ain't at it again? You want to take up Receiving. I'm telling you, strictly legit business.'

'Dean I ain't never done nothing. I was only after getting Noreen her tea — '

'Oh yeah how that cooking going Nicky?'

'Dean I got to get in there. Respect man, and you take care none of them pigs clock them jackets — '

'Nicky you just gob it when you get in there.' We both cackled. He went off get a cab and I went in the nick.

They were expecting.

Usual crowd in there. Someone lost her cat, Wayne Sapsford bailed on daily reporting, geezer grassing up a neighbour breaking the hosepipe ban, young Asian dude on a producer, all his documents pukka only he got stopped for being Asian. Then there was me.

Chingford fucking nick. You went up the nick three in the afternoon in the van, they bailed you about two in the morning and you got to walk home. That is they bailed you at all. You went there make an official complaint and you drew your pension before they heard you out. Friday afternoon always busy when they paid up the grasses, so I heard. Never go down a big nick Friday afternoons. Matter of fact only the second time I ever went in Chingford up the front door.

Only they expected me.

'Nicky Burkett,' Desk Sergeant turned round and said.

'Powers of observation,' I goes.

'DS TT Holdsworth is waiting for you.'

'Thought he was on a bleedin' course. Interpersonal skills.'

'He finished. He got the skills now.'

'Jesus.'

DS Holdsworth they always had him down DS TT Holdsworth on account of he got big wheels. Now he came out the back like he just put them in thirty-fifth gear.

'Nicky! Good to see you! Just like old times!'

'That them interpersonal skills, TT? You got a result there mate, turn round and talk like a fuckin' Yankee.'

Stopped him there like you whacked him. Spun round clocking for his mates find out who was passing the word.

'Bastards,' he went. 'Bastards all of them. They just have to see a feller trying to improve himself, make something of his career structure and what do they do only take the piss.'

'Hard world TT,' I goes.

He pulled himself up. 'Nicky,' he turned round and said, 'come in the back I need to have a chat like.' He pulled up the barrier and we went down the interview room.

'That one of them Chingford chats where I get bounced round the walls then charged Criminal Damage on the paintwork?'

'Ha ha Nicky, you and me we're good friends, you know I wouldn't do that to you. Come to think of it' — he started speaking loud, always got this feeling I was wired and have it round the papers — 'come to think of it we don't do that sort of thing to anyone in this nick. Servants of the community right? Anyway this is more of a cup-of-tea job Nicky, quiet-word situation, man to man.'

'Oh like that?'

'Like that Nicky.'

'Who you wanting fingered then? Kind of dosh you offering make it worth my while?'

'Nicky!' Started wetting himself. 'Nicky it ain't like that.' He came round the table all the same and patted me down for wires being on the safe side. 'There was never any cash in this project, not directly you understand, at least not from us, although there were rewards from other sources.'

I never knew what the fuck he was on about.

'You see Nicky that Chingford MP turned up dead on your doorstep.'

'Fuck all to do with me TT. Your manor Chingford.

Me I'm Walthamstow.'

'You voted in the last election?'

'Never miss. *Reader's Digest*, Littlewoods, American Express, I send 'em all off.'

'Er, yeah. Now like I was saying you know how that MP was on your doorstep.'

'Up the market I was. Buying them Laura Ashley pies. He was like dead on arrival TT.'

'Nicky no one reckons you murdered Oliver Mannion.'

'You sure about that? Old Bill always reckon I murdered everyone TT. Prime suspect. Innocent passer-by situation only they stitch me up like.'

'Nicky you got about a hundred witnesses the last two times you killed someone. Members of the community.' Mentioned that

22

community TT and he looked like he expected a chorus. 'Only we all know you never shafted him this time. Nicky there's something you got to know. I sent him to you, Oliver Mannion.'

'What!'

'I've got to tell you Nicky it was straight up.'

'Straight up!' I got up and walked round and gawped at him. 'Straight fucking up! Excepting you never happened to turn round and tell me about it. Jesus TT.' I was fucking gobsmacked.

'He reckoned he wanted a problem sorted. Could've been a drink in it for you Nicky. Maybe a big drink.'

'Jesus. Wanted a problem sorted. Kind of problem TT?'

'Asked if I could help him out. If I knew anyone could help out with surveillance type of thing. Not a police job. No receipt you understand me?'

'Fucking understand you mate, fucking understand you straight up the fucking platform. And like how you were in this fucking conversation TT? Cocktails up his fucking palace with him or what?'

'That's where the queen lives Nicky. MPs sit up Parliament. Matter of fact it was over the golf course now you come to mention it.

Know how it is when you're both members. Get chatting.'

'Jesus H. fucking Christ and his rabbit.'

'Over a few holes. Tell you the truth Nicky I reckon he fetched me out, thought I might be useful to him.'

'Specially he wanted a spot of that surveillance.'

'Not only that, also in a wider sphere — '

'Like surveilling some geezer with some bleeding machete you reckon?'

'Nicky!'

'Like he knew he was getting surveilled himself so he reckoned he get his surveillance in first or what?'

'Nicky never for one moment — '

'Fuck me round that fuckin' golf course TT, you got any more confidentials or can I fuck off now?'

'Nicky he mentioned he wanted a few people watched. He said he was sure there was a conspiracy against him.'

'He was never too fuckin' wrong then innit?'

'But he didn't want the police involved, or not officially. It was too delicate. So I told him he couldn't have it like that, either it's an official police matter or it isn't.'

'Be a fuckin' first then. So all them back-handers off villains is official you're telling me?'

'So then I thought about it and I put your name up Nicky. Might fit the bill if you'll pardon the expression. Know the manor. Got a few friends. Got a result before. Maybe you could do a bit of security for him, earn yourself a few bob. Find out what his problem is, then maybe the same time you might even like to keep me informed, you understand me . . . ?'

'Easy fucking peasy.'

'Easy peasy Nicky. No problem.'

'So you wanted some geezer sorted — '

'No!'

'Some geezer sorted and you get a back pocket for the intro'. And help the fucking career along. And fit me up. Then me, maybe I get a little drink off it and you reckon you got me for a grass! Jesus TT you reckon I came down off the fucking Christmas tree or what? You reckon I plunge geezers like for practice, keep my fuckin' hand in? You reckon I want to take the fall for some fuckin' MP dickbrain? I got my dole money TT, quite relaxed on forty quid a week. Don't want no geezers brown bread on my doorstep thank you, not even one or fucking two of them.'

'Nicky that was very unfortunate. He said watched. I thought it was a little personal problem. I had no idea. Absolutely no idea at all. I thought I was doing you a favour. Yes, I admit, it'd do my career no harm — '

'TT I give you an official statement. You can fuck off. End of statement. I ain't even signing it. You want me again you check my lawyer.' I went out the corridor and down the front.

Wayne Sapsford still never signed the book. Little Wayne got very frustrated, they kept him many more minutes he was likely for petrol bombing the place.

I went off back Walthamstow. Never did fancy Chingford. Never fancied Chingford Hall where that Kelly used to doss, never fancied Highams Park where she dossed now. In fact never fancied anywhere Kelly dossed. Never liked Chingford nick, never liked Chingford geezers, never liked Chingford fucking Sainsbury's superstore and now I never liked Chingford MPs.

They were all better in Walthamstow even the fucking MP.

I needed an assist. Needed someone for yacking to on all of it. Get an angle. Point of principle you never gave Old Bill cred. They tell you the time and it got to be yesterday's. TT put my name up meant he wanted some geezer whacking, had to be. Even he was telling the truth I still never believed it.

Then he had me down a grass!

I needed a loan of some brain business.

Only first off I went round Mum's.

Mum lived with Shithead up Priory Court, one of the blocks they made into a space station when they renovated. People lived there still drank their tea then pissed it out again only now it was Chingford piss, came out of some arty-farty drive-in fucking super-complex round the other side the North Circular.

Time was I'd lift a jeep out of north Chingford for getting from the nick down Priory Court, only Noreen reckoned I was a dead man next time I lifted a motor, reckoned she'd choke me with her diaphragm middle of the night. Trouble with Noreen was she meant it. Two options then coming out the copshop. Wait for Wayne Sapsford and get a ride off whatever he nicked or catch a bleeding bus with the grannies.

I went with the grannies so it took an hour getting up Priory Court. Stolen motor it only took five minutes. Outside Mum's a silver BMW, stars and moons and shit down the side. No kids tampering with it. Rameez was visiting Sharon.

'Rameez,' I goes indoors.

'All right Nicky? I heard you been causing

them by-elections, know what I mean?'

They were drinking that Safeways own brand. Not only they never shopped local, they went up Safeways miles off. You ever drank that Safeways own brand? I had better sewage.

And Rameez was in my mum's drinking tea. Far as I knew Rameez only got off on three activities. Slicing geezers, sitting in silver motors and putting it up white birds. Drank Pernod on account of it was expected. Now he was on the settee with a cup. And saucer.

'Nicky where you bleedin' been you bleedin' little sod?' goes Mum. 'Rameez was only telling us about you, how it was never true what they said on the news about you killing that MP. You never came round and told your poor old mum you never did it, innit? Bleedin' better not be true I'm telling you. Bleedin' MPs what next eh? Bleedin' newsreaders? Bleedin' weather forecasters?'

'Conservative too,' goes Shithead. 'No bloody respect these days that's the trouble.'

'Such a good boy Rameez,' goes Mum. 'Visits his mum every day. Tells her what he's doing where he's going how his business is getting on . . .'

Rameez shot me a butcher's on the side and we cackled quiet. Business might be protection might be performance motors might be crack and Es. The fuck he told Mum? Sharon was giggling one corner pretending she was playing with the kid. Then again Rameez might have an interest in Sharon's business, visiting massage like she was the radio controller sending the girls round.

'Rameez,' I goes in the passage.

'Nicky.'

'You putting it up our Sharon again?' Rameez's scars were covering up again nicely now, almost looked a normal geezer. Grinned at me, never a pretty sight, generally meant evil.

'Nicky I passed by on a business matter with Sharon. We may have some negotiations later.'

'Say no more mate I never want to know. I only came round for a cup of rosie get out the way a bit, only they're drinking fucking Safeways own brand. You and your boys around? I need an assist.'

'No problem Nicky what the story?'

'Fuck knows. Old Bill reckons the geezer came round mine sort out some problem. I only wondered some other geezer might come round want to tell me what the problem was.'

'Serious matter Nicky. Serious water you

got there. Might need an assist.'

'Yeah. You boys help out with any agg?'

'Always available Nicky you know that. Prefer it we make some paper out of it you understand.'

'Understood, course.' Matter of honour involved, Rameez got loyal as a dog, slice any geezer you wanted. Commercial proposition though, still got to be commercial. No wedge coming in and he got withdrawal. Cold turkey. Turn nasty. Find out there was a point of honour after all, slice you for non-payment.

★ ★ ★

They called a fucking press conference.

On account of a fucking MP got the knockback they reckoned they wanted to explain it to the papers. They were meaning the fucking *Sun* only in the bargain they had to let the long papers in. And why they wanted me there, they were looking for someone to explain it all away.

'Not a fuckin' bonzo,' I went to TT when he like softened me up with the sweet wordings. 'You tell your own fuckin' porkies TT, I ain't doing it for you. Never fuckin' bothered you a whole lot up to now like innit?'

'But you got to give it credibility Nicky,' TT turned round and said. 'Being a member of the public you understand. Innocent and that.'

'No fuckin' bonzo.'

'And if you don't we might have to charge you.'

'The fuck with? Charge me? TT I'm as straight as a monk's cock you know that. Straighter than bleedin' Snow White. Do me a favour TT know what I mean?'

'We'll find something on you Nicky no problem.'

So next day we had their press conference. They told me I got to tell lies from beginning to end.

There was me and the fucking Chief Superintendent, how they got a new one since the last one got an accident. They got some smooth PR bird Caroline and some slippery fucker out of the Home Office name of Elliot, talked like the queen kept offering me backhanders. They got TT. They got their CID Inspector Forrest, first on the scene so he did most of the gabbing. Then they got me.

Forrest reckoned how it all happened. Oliver Mannion got to make a mistake on the address or maybe they dumped him there on a cover-up. Fuck all to do with me, innocent bystander and member of the public.

So then they all came to me.

'Mr Burkett!' they all yelled.

'One at a fuckin' time!' I yelled.

'Nicky,' went the PR bird Caroline, 'this is on live TV.'

'Yeah?'

'Now,' she went to the lads, 'you will all have your question in turn, one question each please. You first.'

She pointed up some fucking wino on one side I reckoned came in out of the cold.

'The *Sun* newspaper,' he went.

'*Sun* ain't a newspaper,' I goes. 'Fuckin' comic innit?'

'Mr Burkett,' he goes, 'would you say Oliver Mannion was a victim of sex games gone wrong or do you have some other explanation for his perversions that he was trying to satisfy at your address?'

'I ain't too fuckin' SP'd up on all that howsyourfather,' I goes. 'Serious mash-up bring down heavy grief on your hoo-ha innit? You get my meaning John-boy?'

'Mr Burkett!' goes next one. 'The *Scotsman!*'

'Who me?'

'Mr Burkett, do you suppose Mr Mannion was coming to see you or do you suppose he was there by accident? Or what else do you suppose was the cause of his being there?'

'Came round by me on account of TT put a drink my way innit?'

'Nicky — ' TT hissed.

'Fuckin' MP only wanted a whacking on some conspiracy stitch-up so he had words on TT here pass a bit of work round. TT put my name up, say no more. Fuckin' housy fuckin' housy.'

'Nicky,' goes some creep in denim reckoned he was Mr Cat. 'The *Guardian*.'

Not *Walthamstow Guardian* neither, I clocked Bridget Tansley on one side.

'Nicky we have heard some speculation here from the police and the Home office as to why Mr Mannion should have been at your address, but we have heard very little about why he might have been murdered. Why do you think it could have been? Was it a drug war? Was he trying to buy votes? Was it sexual jealousy? Can you help us here, from your resonant perspective of street values?'

'Straight up,' I goes.

'Yes?'

'Straight up. You hit it straight on the hammer mate I reckon.'

'Yes?'

'Only one cause you ever get smacked innit? It got to be the gear. Or some bird. Or maybe some piece of dosh or your motor got lifted or you stepping on some geezer's toes or some other reason, you hear what I'm saying?'

'Yes . . . Exactly Nicky, that's very interesting indeed.'

'And we have got to wind it up now!' goes the fucking Super. 'And I hope that answers all your questions!'

'No!' they go.

'Yes!' he goes.

Then we slide out.

After that I never got checked by the papers so much. Maybe they reckoned I helped them out so sweet they never liked to ask up any more favours. Regular geezers respect your private life.

I never got any of that hospitality after, I always heard how they gave out the hospitality when you got on TV. Got to be the cuts.

3

Big fucking bird in shades followed me down the market. And a red hat. Not many of them down Walthamstow market.

Jimmy Foley was retailing some Es outside the Pizza Hut. 'Nicky,' he goes, 'big fucking woman in a red hat's checking you man.'

Elvis Littlejohn posing outside the precinct looking cool held me up. 'Nicky,' he turned round and said, 'your grannie after you man, big fuckin' woman in a red hat's checking you, maybe you never ate your pudding up man.'

Aftab Malik opposite the banana stall. Aftab never spoke only twice a year, preferred whacking geezers. 'Huh Nicky,' he goes. 'Know what I mean.'

'I knows,' I turned round and said.

'Huh.'

There I was going all right to everyone, all right John, all right Maise, all right Asif. Shelley Rosario offering me one round the police hut, Wayne Sapsford left a Fiat up Sainsburys' car park, everyone liming. All of them reckoned there was a big fucking bird in shades and a red hat checking me. I did a bit of that shopping and she was still there. What the fuck?

I got to reason with her, ask her business. Never needed any more shit.

Best place for a mugging round there was the gents' toilet by the bus station. Quiet and slippery, no one ever went in there for a pony. Only she might not come up there. Got to be the library then.

I went in looking for a spot. Upstairs was quiet as a Scousers' art class. She came in, followed me. Religion and sociology, no fucker interested in that one. I hid up waiting.

Never had a weapon with me. Bad practice, always want a weapon. I lifted a bit of shopping out, biggest thing I bought.

She came round the corner the bookcase and I whacked her.

Only way to smack someone with a yam was straight between the mince pies. I smacked her good. She gave a little flutter and started to go down nicely backwards in the aisle. I dragged her across into Punjabi. She clucked and gurgled a bit, kind of concussed. Gave her a rub down make sure she was never tooled up. Clocked her bag. No blade. Nor in her shoes.

'Wha . . . ?' she went vague.

'Shut your gob,' I went.

'Wha . . . ?' she went. 'I can't see.'

'Bit of soil in your beadies, do you no harm,' I goes. 'Now gob up.'

'You're Nicky Burkett,' she goes.

'Shut the fuck up.' How the fuck did I get her out of there?

'I am Diana Mannion.'

'The fuck you are.'

'I am the widow of the murdered man.' Then she faded away like the power went off in your cassette. Shit. Still no one coming into Punjabi, never could pick a better spot for it. I belled Noreen on the mobile.

'Noreen.'

'All right Nicky?'

'Noreen I got a problem.'

'Kettle taking too long to boil? Toast too thin?'

'Noreen I just concussed that MP's missis in religion and sociology up the library.'

Pause.

'Where are you now Nicky?'

'In Punjabi.'

'Don't be a bleedin' idiot Nicky I don't care what section you're in. Still in the library, right?'

'Yeah.'

'What you going to do now?'

'Going to take her back our gaff when she wakes up.'

'Very nice. So what's the problem?'

'You reckon the problem Noreen. You come home and smell woman in there and I'm solo in shit creek innit? Even she's old and that, thirty-five if she's a day, you sniff her and it's garden shears job.'

Noreen started bubbling, sitting down there round her desk playing up the computers getting her little rocks off thinking on my predicament. Birds never did appreciate geezers' problems.

She was still cackling. So bleeding happy at my distress she never even fussed I committed some crime.

'See you later Nicky,' she goes.

I sat down by that Diana Mannion. Big woman. Smelled of sweat and perfume. Reckoned I might give her another rub down. She woke up again.

'You're Nicky Burkett,' she goes again.

'You got to speak Punjabi in this section,' I turned round and said.

'What did you hit me with?'

'I never hit no one lady. You just came over faint. Gave you the mouth-to-mouth, brought you round.'

'You gave me mouth-to-mouth?'

'Good news we did it at school. Knew it'd be handy some day.'

'Well.'

'Seeing as how you're better now after that

first aid maybe I'll fuck off then.'

'No! I need to talk to you.'

'Yeah only you reckon I need to turn round and talk to you lady?'

'My husband came to talk to you.'

'Got interrupted.'

'The police told me my husband came to see you to sort out a problem for him.'

'No lady. Fuck knows what he wanted. I never sort no problems. They start out problems they finish up massacres they come by me.'

'I want you to sort out this problem for me.'

'Lady you got snot dribbling down your mush. Comes of fainting like that. You want to sort out that problem first?'

She went slowly in her bag and got some tissues and dabbed up.

'I want to talk to you. Is there a restaurant or hotel where we can go for a cup of tea perhaps?'

We never had restaurants nor hotels round Walthamstow. Nor was I wanting being clocked with her, never live the fucker down.

'Missis,' I went. 'You go out this library, turn right on to Hoe Street. You cross over there and wait on the corner by the Council. I follows you straight behind. You got it?'

'Help me up.'

Shit.

I got to put my mitts round her, hauled her up felt her tits. Not such a bad experience considering it was a nightmare. Big ones. She leaned her Judge Dread on my shoulder a minute, oh Gawd. Then she braced up and stepped downstairs. Five minutes later I followed her and caught her up on the corner.

★ ★ ★

'You never reach her Nicky anyway.' Noreen still cackling quiet to herself in the kitchen.

'How you reckon that Noreen?'

'About a foot taller than you Nicky, you stand her up against the wall and you need a ladder to poke her.'

Noreen never worried over the bird being two hundred years old, snot all over her and some big bruise on her mug. Only thing stopping me shafting her she reckoned was I was too midgy.

We went back in with the tea. Second cup we had, after the first one she went straight off sleeping on the settee. Noreen came home from work early, clock the action. Bird woke up again. More tea.

'He gave me the mouth-to-mouth technique,' she goes.

'He did?' Noreen's little beadies going big then very, very small. 'You sure?'

'Oh I am sure. He is a fine young man. He will help me.'

'Never known him on the mouth-to-mouth you see lady. Mouth to anything else only not mouth-to-mouth.'

I went back out the kitchen for the toast. When I got back in they were talking woman talk. 'Yeah yeah,' Noreen was going. 'Yeah.' Like she was the listening party this hour. Next hour likely the other way round while she told all about me and the other bird gave with the yeah yeahs. How it goes round.

'My husband was my whole life, he was everything to me,' the bird went. Not the best way for getting to Noreen that, seeing how she always leaned in the antigeezer direction, independence and that. 'How can I live without him?' Then she started leaking and that snot started running down her boat race again. 'He is dead. Dead.'

'And on our bleedin' stairs too,' I goes.

'Someone killed him.'

'Maybe it was an accident,' goes Noreen.

'Now they will want to kill me too I am sure of it. I know too much.'

'What do you know lady?'

'Everything and nothing.'

'Hear what you're saying.'

'Noreen — '

'Yeah?'

'Can I call you Noreen?'

'Best you do,' goes Noreen, 'or I get confused.'

'Can I confide in you Noreen?'

'You want.'

'I am frightened. I want revenge.'

'Yeah.'

'I want to find out who killed my husband. Who killed Oliver.'

'Can we call him Oliver?' I went. Noreen gave me the stare.

'Before they kill me.'

'Yeah.'

'There are people following me. Four men in a car followed me to your home today.'

Cheers.

'Listen Mrs Mannion,' Noreen goes.

'Diana, please, dear.'

'Listen, er, Diana . . . ' Noreen went a bit slow, started giggling on account of we never got many Dianas round our way. 'Listen, Diana, you best leave all that to the Old Bill you know.' Got a blank on that so she started again. 'Er, to the pi . . . to the police force. What they get paid for, police protection innit? And catch them murderers, right?'

'I have no confidence in the police.'

'Right on lady,' I goes. 'No more haven't

we, know what I mean?'

'Do you know why my husband was coming to see you?'

'Fuck knows. In the area, reckoned he'd pop in.'

'He came to you because you were named. He came to you because he thought you could help him unmask the conspiracy against him.'

'Serious work that conspiracy,' I went. 'Get a five for it no problem.'

'Oliver did not tell me himself.' She did a bit of sobbing. 'The police told me that part. Then I read about it in the newspapers. Then I saw your address there as well. So I came . . . ' She started leaking again.

'Brace up woman,' I goes. 'Fuck's sake.'

She breathed in, did a bit more dabbing. 'He chose not to go to the police. He had reasons I know. He was a very, very clever man Oliver. And very, very ambitious. He would not let a minor problem stand in his way . . . '

'You turn round and telling us he wanted to waste them innit?'

'I loved his big ambition . . . ' she blubbed. 'Oh Gawd.'

'I will not go to the police either. I want to do what Oliver wanted to do. I want to start by finding out who my husband thought was conspiring. Whoever conspired against him killed him.'

'Reasonable.'

'And I want to resolve the problem as my husband wanted to resolve the problem. Why he went to you.'

Jesus. She wanted a hitting too? 'Tell her Noreen,' I went.

'Mrs Mannion . . . Diana,' Noreen turned round and said. 'Nicky don't do things like that. Maybe he did used to do them crimes but he don't do them no more. He . . . does cooking and dusting more these days.'

Trust your bird build you up.

'Good God!' she went very quick. 'I did not mean crimes. I want him to investigate, report to me, then inform the police of what he knows . . . '

Likely fucking story.

'Trouble is though lady he don't do that neither you understand. He don't grass up. Against his principles. Maybe he don't like these geezers much, still he probably prefer them to Old Bill you understand me? No offence like but he reckons it's your business, between you and them geezers what happens round your manor you get my meaning? Anyway you don't mix with them criminal types no more innit Nicky?'

'Never,' I goes quick.

'What are your rates?' the bird asks.

'Pardon?'

'I said what are your rates? Weekly, monthly, whatever.'

'We got Council Tax here lady we don't pay them rates no more.'

'Oh dear. What do you charge if I hire you?'

'Yeah but you don't lady.'

'Plus expenses of course. I realize you must have expenses. Taxis, meals, police bribes, that sort of thing.'

'But we don't lady.'

She leaned over and she watered. Seemed like she was well shredded. Seemed like she reckoned they were on her case. Shared cremation with hubbie.

Noreen gave her the sympathy. I got the tequila. They reckoned enough tequila turned your brain like a corkscrew. Maybe enough tequila might set her straight again.

4

Special offer at Pizza Hut two for one, so I was after getting them for the freezer. Extra hot peppers. While they were cooking up I went in Hammick's bookshop next door.

Noreen wanted some book by Terry McMillan, sent me looking before. Last time though I never clocked it so I offered her Terry Venables instead only she never thought that was humorous so I had to go back sharpish. I had a skin round. Minding my own business when just then a shadow came over.

'Well well,' goes Mickey Cousins. 'If it ain't Nicky Burkett reckons he's so fuckin' smart he's reading a book now. Bit of an intellectual eh?' Mickey was bold on account of he got his geezers with him, Tweedledum and fucking Tweedledummer.

'Hold on while I look that up in the dictionary,' I went.

'Been waiting for you Nicky.'

Mickey Cousins been waiting nearly a year, letting the coast die down. Letting his bones mend. Now he came back on the fucking scene. Very fucking handy.

'Yeah? Go wait some other fucking place then Mickey this is a fucking bookshop. You wait in here you got to browse mate. Waiting without browsing, not allowed.' I went over near the till.

He followed.

Good to see he was still limping, nice to know the damage was never temporary.

We got Mickey on his tod that time, round by his gaff when he was coming back from the Chinese. Me and Rameez and Aftab and Afzal. We slapped him hard and we were carrying. Broke his windows and a couple bones.

Question of self-defence natural enough. Mickey was lined up with some big geezers and they wanted to waste us. Did him a favour matter of fact. Next day they got sorted and Mickey wasn't around.

Looked like he never felt the gratitude.

Mickey was a bent car dealer up north Chingford. Performance motors lifted out of Hampstead loaded on the next container out of Tilbury. Or wrecks off the M25 finished up at Mickey's, three motors folded into one, good as new except they broke up when they went over seventy. Mickey wore a camel-hair coat. Got a few bob. They made him a director up the Orient and he wore that coat match days.

'Been waiting a long time for you Nicky Burkett. Payback time. You came in my home.'

'Who me? Some other geezer Mickey. Not me stepping on your toes mate. Live and fucking let live.'

'You came in my home,' he went again. 'You brought business on my doorstep you little fucker. Then you took liberties, hurt me. Now it's payback time. End of fucking story.'

Mickey never moved only one of his animals hit me. Fucking Christ. Short-arm jab had a bit of practice behind it. Tweedledum he got rings on his fingers. My breath left home and blew out somewhere round Leyton. My body hurt like I was having a baby. I cried out loud like they call them to prayer up the mosque.

No problem guessing the next action. He got my hair, pulled up my Judge Dread lined for the butt. Aimed. I heard someone got stiffed off a nose kiss one time. I never liked the forecast at all, called for desperate measures. I yanked on his dick.

Exactly the same moment their assistant manager, nice little bird good body, grabbed him from behind. He went for the spot only he got moved sideways.

He headed that bookshelf right hard. It was never as soft as my hooter.

So there was fucking gravy spraying everywhere, burst all directions straight out his boat race. I never clocked anyone headbutt a bookcase before, very dramatic indeed.

I was out the door.

Next mistake though was going back after my pizza. Problem was that two-for-one offer I never wanted to miss it. Ran up the counter after it. Hardly walk leave alone run, stumbling and moaning and shaking and hawking all the same time. Mickey and fucking Tweedledummer behind. They were so leery now they never cared they iced me in the Pizza Hut. Fucking terrified was never in it. Never mix with hard men unless you got a serious advantage.

Still that bleeding pizza was never cooked. Shit and fuck. I ran down the other side the restaurant. Tweedledummer came through the middle past the salad bar. Salad bar up Pizza Hut was crap, Pizzaland was always better only they never got one up Walthamstow. Still Tweedledummer never ought to put his mitt in the coleslaw shoving past for bringing me down. Mind you they always put the coleslaw in the corner, asking for trouble. Then he took out the waitress bringing round some geezer's top-size pizza, she went down and that pizza went flying all over some other geezer by his solo table sitting there quiet.

Vegetarian special with extra chillies.

Mickey was gone. Came to his senses, knew Old Bill got to be there thirty seconds off the market. Knew his animals were never grassing him up. See them right later on.

I was gone in the bargain. Limped off like I just had an argument with a double decker. Gave up on the pizza for now. Pick it up later. Going in the freezer anyhow, not too sad it was cold.

That vegetarian special with extra chillies landed all over a geezer name of Mervyn. Biker. Mervyn was kind of quiet only you kept in sweet with Mervyn. He got easily roused. Liked his pizza did Mervyn only probably not all down his front, peppers in his balls. He looked up kind of gentle.

Maybe Old Bill got there in time or maybe Tweedledummer was a dead man.

I was gone.

★　★　★

Down the marshes round the back of Tudor Court they got blackberry bushes. Supposed to be they banned you going there on account of some fucking thing round the dump they put there. Radiation or nuclear waste and that. It got peaceful down there though so I

50

went there for a bit of hush and picking some blackberries. Jump over the stream and there was me and the rabbits.

Never did work out the fucking season for blackberries. Worked on the rule if they were never there it was no grief, if they grew then I got a result. One thing you got in London though, blackberries they grew big and hairy. Countryside they never got hairs on them, we reckoned that one time we went in the country after them. Or maybe it was that radiation.

Wanted to make Noreen a blackberry pie. Made her one before and she put me down as Mr Special, gave me it there and then on the settee like there was no tomorrow. Right in the middle she turned round and said it was that molasses sugar did it, made her feeling so sweet. Only she had a problem turning round and saying it on account of she kept giggling and coming, coming and giggling. Me I put it down to the blackberries. Reckoned I might need all the help I could get for keeping her sweet when I told her Mickey Cousins never wanted to kiss and fucking make up.

Mickey's mates gave Noreen her little thin scar down her jaw, Stanley knife, six inches. I got very happy indeed when we slapped Mickey.

Fucking blackberries never grew. Maybe

December was too early. I pissed off round Mrs Shillingford's instead, see she got any ideas.

★ ★ ★

Mrs Shillingford was a bit old like ninety-two. Blind as a bleeding bat and got that arthritis, never got her specs when she needed them and never could get after them on account of the arthritis. Always belled her first unless she was expecting me, then waited half the afternoon for her answering. She never answered the door without her specs on.

'Mrs Shillingford. Got a problem. I pop round a minute?'

'Of course you can Nicky dear it would be a pleasure.'

Made my way up Greenleaf Road.

Sundays I went round Mrs Shillingford's when I never committed crimes that week. She taught me that cooking. I went round there Sundays for cooking her meal and tidying up a bit. Belled her Fridays told her I was passing the test keeping my hooter clean. Then a couple times I had to cancel Saturdays when an opportunity came up only generally things stayed regular. Then after Noreen decided she was my bird she used to go round Mrs Shillingford's Saturdays in the bargain. Only got her a snack Saturdays on account of there was no time for a meal between the yacking. Yacked six hours solid how women do. Twelve till six then Noreen came home with a thirst on. Poor old Mrs Shillingford probably went straight to her pit shagged out.

After Noreen made her moves on me I was round Mrs Shillingford's near every week anyway. Noreen reckoned any more of that stupidness and she was away on her toes. So I stopped committing villainies so I went round Mrs Shillingford's for dinner.

Sundays we took it slow. Bit of grub, bit of rum and then Mrs Shillingford yacked about when she was a kid back in Dominica. Seventy-eighty years ago she reckoned they still got plenty action specially round Carnival time. On that subject I was after a bit of advice.

'Come in Nicky dear,' she shouted out. 'Come in it is not locked.' Some reason Mrs Shillingford reckoned on account of she was near as blind then everyone else got deaf. Had the box on full volume, same difference. Now she got the racing on.

'All right Mrs Shillingford? You got money down or what?'

'I have a small wager on this one with my accountant, yes.' She always reckoned the geezer she belled was her accountant, called him Mr Ladbroke. Shouted at him she wanted 10p on the nose.

'They be sending a barrow round with the dosh any minute I expect then Mrs Shillingford.'

'Nicky be a good boy and find my spectacles then we can watch this race in peace.' Meaning shut the fuck up a minute. She never could clock the TV even she got ten pairs of specs.

Geegee came in fifth.

'I expect it was rigged again,' she goes. 'You know they give them a big drink of water just before the race when they want them to lose. Oh thank you Nicky.' While she was watching the nags going round I was making her some of her lemon tea.

'Mrs Shillingford you got to give me a touch for that Noreen tonight.'

'You have not upset her Nicky? You have not been chasing those other girls again?'

'Again? What's that again Mrs Shilling-ford?'

She cackled. 'I know your sort you see Nicky. Men you know they do always like a bit of muffin on the side as you say. Always.'

'Mrs Shillingford I do that to Noreen and she cut it off I telling you. Anyhow like you were saying you was never any different back in them days innit?'

'Well . . . ' She started the thinking.

'Mrs Shillingford that Mickey Cousins is back in the frame.'

'Oh dear. That man.'

'Came after me today right unfriendly. Noreen ain't never going to be happy about it. Fact is she could be considerable upset, know what I mean? Want to do something make her sweet. Only I been round the marshes and there weren't no blackberries.'

Mrs Shillingford knew that part the story off me. Probably she knew the rest off Noreen down to every little jerk and spurt. How it goes.

'I see. You are such a good boy Nicky. Most of the time.'

'You got to tell me what it was used to get you going Mrs Shillingford. Back then when you were a young bit and you got back in them bushes with some young dude, you get my meaning? What it was made you feel kind of nice. What I could be getting for that Noreen like.'

'Bush, Nicky, bush. I be telling you it was not bushes in Dominica. We went out in the bush.'

'Oh yeah.'

So she started on the thinking. Then she started on the chuckles, kind of slow heavy chuckles on account of cackling too quick made to hurt on the old arthritis.

'I reckon you remembered then,' I turned round and said.

'Yes I remembered Nicky. You are a bad boy after all you know making me remember these things. It is not good for my ailments.'

'Get away with you Mrs Shillingford you be bouncing around after I gone now you remembered all that.'

'I am telling you Nicky. I do have the recipe for some niceness I do believe. I do have it.'

'What I'm after, you hear what I'm saying.'

She stopped a bit then she worked it out. Then she blushed all coy. 'I think,' she went slow, 'I think you should take some ripe bananas.'

'Yeah?'

'Back home we have many sorts of bananas but to you they will be only bananas I know. Take some ripe bananas.'

'Bananas.'

'You place them in the oven and then you bake them until they are black.'

'Black.'

'Then you take them out of the oven.' She went all misty while she gave it the memory. 'Then you cut them open down the side so they are all soft and inviting.'

'Bit like that Noreen.'

She smacked me.

'Then you pour in some rum. You may prefer brandy. We also used sweetened milk on it but you should try cream. You spread the brandy and cream all over, I am telling you all over those bananas. Then you eat them.'

'Jesus Mrs Shillingford I reckon you got a result there innit? You reckon we got to have a trial run here see I don't never make any mistakes just screw it up? You got my juices going giving it the picture, what it does to that Noreen.'

She cackled. 'No Nicky, you go and make it now and then if it goes well you can make it for me on Sunday when you are coming. You can come on Sunday? You have not been committing any murders or other crimes I am hoping?'

'Mrs Shillingford not only I not wanting to let you down like, you got to understand I commit any of them bits of work and that Noreen she take them short and curlies and she mash them right up, put them on her dresser for ornaments, know what I mean? Living in fear I'm telling you, living in fear.'

'She is a good girl.'

So I went off for getting bananas.

★ ★ ★

Jimmy Foley was drinking Guinness up The Coffee House by the entrance to the precinct. He bought a cup of tea only it sat there while he drank the Guinness he just lifted out of Food Giant.

I got the bananas out of Food Giant on account of Mrs Shillingford liked me getting them there, Windward Isles bananas. She told me I never steal them, probably came off her family. Then again Noreen told me never steal them so long as I wanted any nookie. All told it was a fucking sight simpler paying up front so I got out the dosh for five pounds of Windwards.

Jimmy Foley was up the cash paying for a jar of that Ragu sauce. Down his inside pockets he got six cans of Guinness he was lifting. The fuck Jimmy reckoned he was going to do with that Ragu was a question. Maybe liked the colour. Took so long checking out the security he never clocked I was behind him. Then he went out and the little Asian bird on the till was a touch of a knee trembler so I just finished chatting her and getting nowhere then I went looking for Jimmy, hear the news. By then he was down The Coffee House.

'Yo Jimmy,' I goes joining him on his table. 'Reckoned you be drinking that Ragu sauce mate stead of that tea you got there.'

'Yo Nicky. The fuck sauce is that?'

'Maybe escaped your notice Jimmy only you purchased one bottle of sauce up Food Giant. Purchased like gave them lettuce for it. In between the serious business. Called Ragu I do believe. In your carrier.'

'The fuck.' Picked it out and beadied it. 'The fuck you do with that?'

'Fuck knows Jimmy. Some kind Italian stuff, put it on their pizza I reckon, extra topping. Goes well with Guinness so I heard.'

'It does?' Jimmy never was top of the bleeding class at school. 'Nicky you in Food Giant?'

'Clocked you committing that theft shop-lifting Jimmy. Bang to rights. Theft times six on account of you got six cans. Just on my road up Walthamstow nick, grass you up get a reward.'

Only then two foreigners came in. Never out of Walthamstow maybe Mile End. Got the gear, big boots and matching haircuts. Two more waiting outside.

This was serious agg.

They came and stood by us, smelling. 'You Nicky Burkett?' went the first one.

'Jimmy here,' I goes. 'He's Nicky Burkett.'

'You Nicky Burkett?' goes his mate to Jimmy. Battle of the masterminds.

'The fuck,' Jimmy turns round and says.

59

He never did forget how he got shot that time sitting down with me. Some reason never get it out his mind.

One of them pulled out a blade.

Shit.

Jimmy picked up his chair and planted it. Quick as a fuck it was over the geezer's skull, fucking fast thinking for Jimmy. Geezer went down.

His mate was round the table, customers scattering. Two outside came after. First one brought his boot up Jimmy's knee and he went over. I was on the geezer from behind. Got salt off the table on my mitts then drilled both of them in his jam pies. Then I was away off him quick waiting the other two fuckers.

Only they never got there.

Just down the hall Paulette James did a favour up the sports shop. Went to school with us that Paulette only now she did that running for England. Always could run quicker than me got to admit it. Very strong bird. Now she was about walking out the precinct down the bus station. Elvis Little-john keeping her company. About a year now Elvis was trying for getting in her knickers. Got as far as rubbing up on her Lycra. Reckoned he was Denzel did Elvis, never could grasp how Paulette was giving him the good friends. They were headed for the bus station together. Clocked me and Jimmy in difficulties.

In the bargain they clocked the difficulties started round two geezers looked like BNP out of Mile End. Elvis and Paulette both black, never got much good news off the BNP. They made their moves.

Elvis did martial arts kicked the geezer up the throat. Paulette was a big strong bird. Geezer already pulled out his bat. Paulette caught it behind and yanked. Geezer never let go, big mistake. That yank off Paulette left him shooting back the hall where he just came from. Straight in the way of security just arriving.

Old Bill not far behind.

On their side one blade, two bats and a couple snooker balls. On our side one jar Ragu sauce. You reckon not much problem sorting out who were the bad hats here.

Took Old Bill five hours and another trip up Chingford fucking nick. Always excepting Paulette course, seeing as she was famous.

And another fucking time I belled Noreen at work, this time out of the cop shop. Told her we got Paulette and Elvis and Jimmy round for bananas that night. Rest was a secret I turned round and said. And first off I got to be questioned.

She made one unhappy noise.

Then I went in a fucking cell again while they sorted it out. Not one pleased geezer.

★ ★ ★

Then they banged me up without even a fucking paper. About an hour I shouted by the door then they brought the *Guardian*. I went how I wanted the *Walthamstow Guardian* not some fucking *Chingford Guardian* no way, so what did they chuck me only the fucking national *Guardian*. Taking the piss here. Fuck knows where they got it, maybe nicked some professor.

So I went back and lay on their bench. One thing you never want to do in a cell is too much of that thinking. Definite brain fever. You got to keep occupied. So I had me a little snooze. Some geezers sleep all the way through a sentence. So I had me a little snooze, then I woke up again. Problem with what to do next so I took the best road out of there. Concentrated on that Noreen's tits.

Not straight off mind, you got to get foreplay. Started the top of her bonce. Worked down her mince pies, hooter, gob, chin, neck, tits. Dwelled round there about twenty minutes, ten minutes left tit ten minutes right tit. Had a good time. Only she was after getting impatient now so I reckoned no good stopping on the tits, best be moving on.

Ribs, belly, fit and a bit round.

Down one side, down the other, then she moved her knees up and there she was waiting for me. Examined her like I was a straight up fanny quack. 'Excuse me,' I goes, 'I am a qualified gyno and I got to make an urgent inspection.' Parked there quite a while on account of I got a resident's permit. Then I reckoned it was time for moving on.

Great thighs Noreen, she always went on how they were too stocky only I marked them fit and strong. Knees not too dusty. Calves like . . .

Two hours and they brought a cup of tea. Piss as usual. I got to make a decision. Bored with that Noreen so I got to be playing away. Whitney Houston or Bridget Tansley off the paper or Paulette James or big blonde PC Burns?

I settled for PC Burns.

Skipped her boat race never her greatest feature. Shoulders a bit bulky specially in that uniform so we took it off. Just getting to work on that fucking great left tit, always was a left tit man first.

They opened the door. 'Fuck off,' I went. 'Just enjoying myself here.'

'You want your property back,' went the Custody Sergeant up the desk.

Packet of Rizlas held a bit of weed, hardly enough one smoke. They ignored it so I got a touch on that one.

'No charges,' goes the pig. 'Hard to believe only you seem to be the innocent party. So you are no longer in custody but first we would be grateful for a witness statement.'

'Sir,' I goes.

'Eh?'

'Innocent party,' I goes, 'so you call me sir innit?'

'Fuck off,' he goes. No respect at all.

'Then,' he turns round and says, 'DSTT Holdsworth wants to have a word in your ear.'

'Take me back in the cell,' I goes.

They took that statement very slow on lined paper.

Two young pigs bright as each other.

'I was passing through Selborne Walk precinct,' it turned round and said, 'on the day in question when I clocked my friend James Foley sitting in The Coffee House drinking a cup of tea. I joined him. 'Yo James,' I went. 'Yo Nicky,' he turned round and said. 'What have you just been buying in Food Giant?' I asked. 'It looks like a jar of Ragu sauce. What are you going to do with that?' 'I am going to make various dishes of Italian cuisine,' he turned round and said.

'Just then two young white men entered the caff who resembled Mile End intellectuals. Without any howsyourfather they immediately launched an affray at myself and James. Under the apprehension that he was myself they attacked him with a bladed instrument. Fortunately one of them fell over a chair and the other developed an eye infection. Two of their supporters were restrained by innocent passer-bys until just then security arrived on the scene.'

Nothing in it I ever wrote only Old Bill made it up same as usual. I signed it.

TT was waiting in the corridor like a virus you never shook off. 'Nicky,' he went all friendly following me out the nick. 'Fancy a quick half then mate eh?' TT always reckoned on account of he was CID he got to meet geezers up boozers.

'Not with you fucker,' I turned round and said. 'Any road, you changed into a bird or what drinking halves? And there ain't a boozer worth the name up Chingford innit?'

'Give you a ride home?'

Now we were talking. 'You ain't got your two-wheeler I hope?'

'I brought the BMW today.'

True as I stood there, TT got a BMW. Reckoned he was a black geezer maybe, Black Man's Wheels. Only TT's wheels were new wheels, not like black geezers' round Walthamstow.

'Backhanders got to be better than they let on TT. Or you been flogging gear off the property officer again? Never did get my Rolex back they took off me one time.'

'Was that a genuine Rolex Nicky or was it a fake?'

'One or the fucking other. Why they keep sending you to yack with me TT?' We were going down Larkshall Road in his fucking BMW, back towards civilization round Walthamstow.

'They think you'll talk to me Nicky.'

'The fuck they get that idea?'

'They get these ideas, inspectors and that. What they get paid for, it don't have to make any sense. Anyway Nicky they get a bit brassed off with you only talking to George Marshall just because he's your warrant officer. And seeing that since they got restructured he's not even in the police force, he chose to stay there so he's a frigging civilian.'

'Maybe accounts for him being a straight geezer.'

'So they reckoned you might like to turn round and tell me how you got into two incidents one after the other, first one in the bookshop then one in Selborne Walk.'

'You find that out TT you fucking give me the news,' I goes. 'Minding my own business and fucking war breaks out is all.'

'Buying a book? Minding your own business buying a book? Got to be for Noreen then, ain't that right?'

'Fuck off copper. Yeah, matter of fact for Noreen. What about that cup of coffee I was after by Jimmy, that for Noreen in the bargain?'

'Diamond girl that Noreen Nicky. Done you the world.'

'Oh fuck's sake TT, get in that boozer eh?'

He parked on a yellow line then we went in the College Arms. Some reason TT always hit the College, reckoned it marked him a thinker probably. Pint of lager.

'Those two villains out of the bookshop Nicky.'

'You got them?'

'The first one broke his nose on a bookshelf Nicky you might have heard. The second one got both ears torn off.'

'Jesus.' So Mervyn got very cross getting his pizza disturbed. Both lugs though was a bit strong, might have settled for one.

'They anything to do with Mickey Cousins?' TT went.

'That Mickey Cousins up Chingford? That Mickey was best mates with your bent super?'

'Leave it out Nicky, you know which Mickey Cousins we're talking here. They connected?'

'Could be I suppose. Never looked a lot like Chingford geezers though. Bit on the bright side.'

'And those other geezers, four of them, they connected with Mickey too?'

'What this 'Mickey too' shit TT? Fuck knows who the fuck they were. Never clocked the geezers before. All I knows is I was drinking a coffee with my mate — '

'Your mate Jimmy Foley.'

'My mate Jimmy Foley, you got a problem with that? Then these four dildos come in got a serious attitude problem towards us. Fortunately they got interrupted.'

'Yes?'

'Yeah.'

'Your round Nicky I think.'

'Having a laugh aintcha? You makin' joke here TT? You serious reckon I buying fuckin' Old Bill a drink? Not now not never. Bad enough get spotted with you, bring out serious quarantine problems. Anyway you be over the limit in that Kraut motor innit?'

'I could have a half.'

'You can fucking buy it in the bargain mate. And no you won't get nothing in exchange. Go talk to your straight up grass over there.'

'Eh?'

Sitting down the corner was little Singing Simpson, Andrew Simpson worked up the snooker hall. Best retailer on the news scene since they closed that secondhand shop Old Bill set up themselves on Hoe Street. They reckoned they nicked all the burglars there fencing the gear. Only problem was half the burglaries only got committed for supplying that shop, fucking Old Bill in disguise fair begged the kids for cassettes and videos. 'Jesus Nicky how — '

'Do me a favour TT, every fucker knows little fucking Singing Simpson. See you around if I don't see you coming.'

I was out of there.

5

We got generous with the rum on our bananas. Came out the oven black as coal. We laid them on our plates three each, me and Noreen and Jimmy and Paulette and Elvis. We got the cream ready.

'What we do again?' goes Elvis.

'Slit them open Mrs Shillingford reckoned,' I turned round and said. 'Then they sit there looking up at you.'

Matter of fact we already got generous with that rum before the bananas ever came out the oven. Paulette reckoned she was allowed three large ones on her training programme, part the relaxation schedule. Anyway she reckoned cannabis showed up on the drug test only alcohol never did. That cream though, she went no way. Stick to bananas and rum.

We drank most the bottle by now.

We made our slit down the bananas. Then we just gawped. No problem clocking what Mrs Shillingford was on about. Soft and gooey they were, laying there open just asking for it. You wanted to stick your finger in.

Noreen and Paulette started giggling. Elvis

reckoned he never believed his luck, Paulette got to give him the long jump after that. Paulette looked like that banana was better than a massage off an international pole vaulter. Noreen gave me one of her little smirks meant I was never going to get any kip. Bleeding amazing bird Noreen only some birds never understood how a geezer got to get a bit of kip after. Clocking that banana I was never sure I was happy or sad.

All meant nothing to Jimmy. Bananas and rum only meant bananas and rum to Jimmy. Good nosh. He stuck his tongue right in it only he stuck it in then pulled it out again concentrating on the process. Jimmy's world you concentrated one thing at a time.

He took his tongue out, started a new thinking. 'Nicky,' he went, 'how come when I get with you there's all geezers wanting to mash me up?'

'Never account for it Jimmy.'

'You remember that time I got shot sitting next to you?'

'Can't hardly turn round and say I do Jimmy, you never mentioned it before. You sure it was you?'

'Sure it was me? You wanna see my exit wound?'

'No no!' everyone went. Then 'yeah yeah!' they all went cackling, changing their mind.

Jimmy got up for doing his party piece, show his entrance and exit. Half Walthamstow clocked his bleeding exit wound.

'Got my exit wound drinking one pint of Guinness,' goes Jimmy. 'Only sitting there drinking one pint of Guinness. Well out of order you ask me.'

'Any other reason?' goes Elvis. 'Or that geezer never liked Guinness?' Elvis knowing the story backward like everyone else only wanting to wind Jimmy up.

'Geezer never fond of Nicky. Plenty geezers never fond of Nicky you reckon. Never fond then, never fond now. This time bring a blade with them up the precinct. Only this time we sorted them innit?'

'Nicky,' Noreen turned round and said thoughtful. 'You think them ones was from Mickey Cousins for sure?'

'What you reckon?' So she made the connection as well.

'They never seemed like Mickey's type. Bit too young, what you say. You think someone rented them out?'

We all drank that rum and gave it brain. Least we all tried only most the brain was on other things and Jimmy never got one anyway. We were pissed up legless and starting to work on a touch of the other. So it got difficult thinking.

'Nicky,' she turned round and said.

'Uh.'

'Nicky you know how it is a girl gets worked up sometimes.'

'Uh.'

'Nicky you awake?'

'Nah.'

'Nicky you got to know you started me all hot and bothered now. Getting them hot flushes for sure. You know the cure for that?'

'Cold shower Noreen.'

'We ain't got a shower Nicky. And I heard the cure was to get a good man, kept on going till he satisfied a girl. You heard that?'

'Nah.'

'You know any good men around Nicky?'

'Ain't none left Noreen you know that. Men's useless like a TV without an aerial you turned round and told me that.'

'May be true Nicky only they still sometimes got their uses Nicky you got to know that. Two good uses I can think of, you want to hear them?'

'Nah.'

'One they can get them things down off the top shelf. Never know when that comes in useful. Two they can give a girl a good rousting once in a while, what you think of that?'

'Gawd.'

Bleeding two o'clock in the morning. We already did it up and down and side to side and follow the leader and round the houses. I was cream crackered. Now she breathing round my fifth gear and licking up my neck, little tongue flicking round all over. She was so bleeding beautiful that Noreen she moved like her pants were full of honey. She got me going again. When her little belly came up around my shoulders I wanted to shout out.

'Noreen you're a bleedin' little tart you know that?'

'I know.'

'Barefaced little cow.'

'Yeah it's true.'

'Come over here.'

'I'm over here already Nicky.'

'So you bleedin' are. Give me that tit of yours for starters.'

'Which one Nicky?'

'Left, course. Same as usual.'

She came across with her left tit.

★　★　★

I belled that Diana off the number on the card she left. Belled her from a callbox, safety rules.

'Hullo,' she went slow. Drink or gear or the doc pilled her up.

'You that Diana?'

'This is Diana Mannion.'

'This here's Nicky Burkett.'

'Yes . . . I remember.'

'Lady things is happening. We got to talk business.'

'Good . . . good. Yes, talk. But I do not want to go to Walthamstow Nicky Burkett. I think you should come here, don't you?'

'Chingford?' I never recognized the dial code on the card. 'No great lover of Chingford lady, never did me no favours specially up north Chingford, you hear what I'm saying?'

'Good God no, not Chingford,' she goes. 'Chingford is full of little men on the make and their ghastly blonde wives. You should come up to our home.'

'You give me a clue where that is or what?'

'Oh . . . oh I see. It is in Hertfordshire of course.' She never said the 't' in Hertfordshire some reason. 'Let me give you the address. Oh, you do drive I suppose?'

'Yeah I drive lady. Not quite the same having a licence though, innit? Minor problem.'

She was never listening. 'Yes . . . ' she went. Then she read out some address up some place I never heard of she reckoned was up the A10 some fucking place. Not on a bus route no danger.

'Come up for a drink and we shall talk.'

'Any time special or I just come?'

'Well, six o'clock. Before dinner.'

'I bring my mate.'

★　★　★

Around teatime Jimmy was shouting outside on the street. 'Yo Nicky!' he calls out, never getting out his motor.

I clocked him out the window.

Jesus.

Jimmy sitting there in a Range Rover on Howard Road.

'Jimmy,' I went, 'park that fucker round the corner, never mind them residents' permits, get up here like.'

'Right Nicky.'

I put the kettle on and lit some weed calm me down a bit. 'Jimmy,' I goes when he settled. 'Where you get that Range Rover?'

'Snaresbrook Jimmy. Some brief left it outside them courts. One car park they never check outside them courts. No problem.'

'You ever clocked one of them Range Rovers on Howard Road before Jimmy?'

'Nah. Can't turn round and say I have

Nicky. We got a result though, best motor for the job innit? Country motor like they all got up the country, know what I mean?'

'And you reckon how many miles they do for the gallon?'

'About twelve I heard Nicky. No problem though I just retailed the stereo out of it, down the snooker hall pay for the petrol. Easy peasy, hear what I'm saying?'

'Jimmy,' I turned round and said.

'Nicky.'

'You a good mate you know that innit?'

'Yeah Nicky. Got shot for you.'

'You reckon where we headed?'

'Country Nicky. Past Chingford. You knowing the land?'

'Fuck knows Jimmy. Only leave alone the country just now, you reckon how we get past Chingford in that motor?'

'Up Waltham Way innit? Sewardstone Road?'

'Jimmy you reckon us wheeling through Chingford in a fuckin' Range Rover? Two boys out of Walthamstow, short hair, one got the criminal viz, other done a six for manslaughter? Then in the country you think on that?'

'Least we ain't black Nicky. Black be a problem. Where exact we going anyway? I need boots?'

'Some place Hadham she reckon. Ain't on my A–Z. You got a map?'

'Yeah that Range Rover got a book. Brought it with me no problem.'

He took out that book, got maps all through it. Neither of us ever much cop on maps. Kept turning the pages never found it that way at all. Looked up Hadham in that index. Kneeling down the floor we got the page then got the square. I went pale.

'Jesus Jimmy . . . '

'Nicky what is it? Nicky you look like you got the heart pox. What you hit on?'

'Jimmy that Hadham you reckon . . . you reckon . . . fuck me only it over the M25!'

'Nah!'

'Telling you Jimmy, see you here. Past that M25. Fucking near Leeds got to be.'

'Jesus Nicky. Primitive up there man. I fuckin' hate them Leeds bastards.' Jimmy always went up West Ham for the Leeds match, smack a few. 'Likely snowing up there too Nicky.'

'Best keep away.'

I belled that Diana again. She sounded like she just came round from another nap. 'You best come down here,' I goes. 'We got a legality problem. Me I never got a licence. Jimmy he's my minder he got to lift a Range Rover come up your way. Against the law.

And you being that MP's missis. Or used to be.'

'What . . . '

She came down Walthamstow. She never liked it, seemed to reckon she got a problem might get whacked with a yam again. Only she came.

We had a meeting.

★ ★ ★

Geezers suffered with that constipation, had to be the Tamil gaff sort you out. You suffered from the cold or a sinus or that angina, still had to be the Tamil gaff. Clear all your passages out goodstyle. They reckoned the Tamils took all your dosh straight back gave it up the Tigers, make a few bombs. Better off they gave someone one of their curries. Start them running straight off.

One time I got one curry up the Tamil gaff. Hiccups lasted two days and sweating a fortnight. See in the dark and grew hairs on my toes. After that I left off the curries, stuck to a bit of dhal and a few cakes. Still curried only they remembered never throwing the whole pepper tree in there.

Diana just got to climb off the train round Tottenham Hale, grab that tube then toddle up Hoe Street out of Walthamstow Central. I

79

had to cut over the patch a couple of minutes off Howard Road. Seemed fair enough.

She was late. Then when she came she was zonked.

Sitting there gabbing with Jimmy on our third cup of tea and little round pattie. Some reason they took *The Times* in there for the customers, Jimmy just reading the stock market report, very interesting, running his thumb under the words.

'Nicky,' he goes. 'It reckons you got to buy an island, good investment, safe as houses. You heard that? You want to buy an island Nicky?'

'Fuck knows Jimmy. Isle of Dogs maybe. Here she coming?'

That Diana she poked her mince pies round the door then she clocked us then she came in a bit unsteady. Yeah she was on the pills. Not likely she got any barbs so she probably had a jar of cheer-ups. Sat beside a bottle of gin.

She grinned at us leery. 'Oh my!' she went slow. 'Oh my!' Grinned again. Grinned up the counter staff. Grinned round the customers except there weren't any.

'Your what lady?' goes Jimmy.

'This is the real culture is it not?' she goes. 'I remember when I was a young girl up country in Kandy we had a wonderful,

wonderful, wonderful time playing hide and seek with our ayah . . . '

'You wanna sit down?' I went. 'Before the life story?'

She went in that chair like a sack of carrots.

Then she blubbed. 'With you Nicky,' she went, 'and Noreen your wonderful, er, girlfriend . . . partner . . . spouse . . . '

'Bird.'

'Your wonderful bird, with you I am having such a lustrous time in the suburbs that sometimes I can scarcely recall my dreadful bereave . . . oh God.'

'The fuck she on about Nicky?' goes Jimmy.

'Lady,' I went, 'this here's Jimmy. My mate. Gives me grief.'

'Jimmy,' she turned round and said, 'we are very pleased to meet you.'

'Lady,' I tried again. 'I reckon we got a problem here.'

'Yes.'

We got three problems. We got number one problem some fucker whacked her Oliver then got her followed up round by me then tried for giving me a small lesson down Selborne Walk. Then we got number two problem Mickey Cousins reckoned he was on a payback the same time, some kind of happy coincidence. Then we got number three problem a crying woman, hard to reason with. Three problems.

'You got to stop leaking lady. Never do the bleeding business.'

'My husband . . . '

'Your husband got whacked. Very sorry. Plenty more geezers though innit? Your problem now is they come after you.'

She carried on leaking. So much for me being sympathetic. 'Oh my God,' she went. 'I'm sorry Nicky. And Jimmy. And everybody. I'm sorry.' She carried on being sorry a time. Then she sat up a bit straighter. Shook her hair. 'Do you have a tissue?' she went.

'We got to turn round and talk.'

'It is good to talk.'

'Someone never likes you.'

She shook her hair again. 'I know.'

'Someone never made you top of their Christmas card list.'

'No. Yes.' She waved up the Tamil geezers. They waved back. She was wanting a tissue off them only she never understood you waved at them round there and they brought tea. No call for tissues. No point even mentioning the subject on account of they never spoke English. You pointed up the counter they brought curry and cake. Aside from that they brought tea.

'My man!' she called.

'My man!' goes Jimmy, meant something different round our way.

'Chai!' went the Tamil geezer. I never remembered his name, they all started on a K then went on the rest of the afternoon. 'Yes!' He went out in the kitchen for the tea and just then things started arriving off the street.

Three big geezers. Blocked the light out. Three geezers never came in for a plate of dhal and three spoons. Nor for reading *The Times*. Fact was they were in such a rush they saved time opening the door, smacked it off the jamb instead. Maybe they were after catching the shops before closing.

'Shit and fuck,' goes Jimmy.

I was out the dining room heading up the kitchen before they smelled me. Door out the back I wanted.

Diana stood up maybe reckoned they brought her tissues. Then she lay down again after she got her jaw broke. Geezers were boxers. Mickey Cousins got them off a gym down Stratford. Recognized one of them, hard man name of Nellie.

I turned round and said it before. Never mix with hard men.

Even Jimmy cottoned that one only it took a bit of time on his thoughts getting down by his legs. Before his legs got moving up the kitchen he found a boot up his back. Lay down.

I was gone.

Then the shooting started.

Then it went quiet.

★ ★ ★

Five minutes and I stepped back off the yard, everywhere quiet. Two Tamil geezers down the floor in the kitchen, one more down the floor behind the counter never moving, practising for being dead. Then it stopped being quiet when the moaning started.

There was Jimmy moaning by the counter, gasping cursing trying to stand up, spot of kidney trouble and a bang on the bonce.

There was Diana moaning groaning crying like you do when your jaw got mash up. She was lying by her chair.

Then there were two big boxers got shotgun wounds. One in the back so he moaned and bled and reckoned he was going to croak. The other up the arse. Not moaning more screaming.

Third geezer lying there quiet got whacked with something.

There was plaster dripping off the ceiling where not all the shots went in the geezers. There was blood dripping off the geezers.

There was tears and dribble and snot dripping off that Diana.

'Fuck,' I turned round and said.

Boxers came after me, got to be. Mickey's type of geezer was Nellie. Teach me a smacking.

Only they stood in some other posse's bit of work. Some other posse got to be after Diana. Carried sawnoffs. Very serious geezers got a very strict attitude.

They gave the boxers our shooting. Stood in their path, got sprayed.

I felt lucky. Jimmy not quite so lucky, never was lucky was Jimmy. Diana not big on the fortune these days either, best stay off the lottery a couple weeks. I was one lucky fucker.

Then Old Bill arrived in spades.

Reckoned it was all my fault natural.

We went up Chingford again for some more of the statements. Belled Noreen again told her I was late home. Listened her digging me out. She was well vex. I was never very over the fucking moon either.

Shit and fuck.

6

It was time for getting out of Walthamstow.
Even a couple days being gone for lifting the
pressure.

'Noreen,' I turned round and said, 'where
you want to go for the weekend?'

'You want to get away Nicky?'

'Fucking right. Somewhere no stupidness
no one on my case no one wants to slice me
up. What you reckon?'

She gave it brain.

'Nicky,' she went narrow-eyed. Always a
bad sign Noreen went narrow-eyed. Never
meant any good for a geezer. 'Nicky,' she went
on when I never answered. 'You know how
you always reading that football magazine?'

'Football magazine?' I goes innocent,
clocking her game plan. 'I never takes no
football magazine.'

'You don't be so bleeding clever Nicky,' she
goes, 'you know what I mean. That magazine
in French.'

'Oh that,' I turned round and said. 'Oh
that.'

'Yeah that.'

'General sport book that. *L'Équipe*. Not

86

just football Noreen.'

'And you takes it on account of you speak French.'

'Well . . . '

'No wells Nicky.'

'Well . . . '

'So we go up Paris the weekend.'

'Noreen!'

'No Noreens Nicky.'

'Noreen be fair!'

'And none of them fairs neither Nicky.'

She knew how West Ham were playing the Scousers Sunday afternoon. So she knew how I reckoned on getting away the weekend then coming back Sunday dinner time, assuming we went up Southend or Margate. Quick as shit she was. Then again she still reckoned I got a few bob stashed from my criminal exploits, how she called them. Counted on finding out where. Put it past Noreen for giving the dosh back Comet Warehouses. 'Shit . . . ' I went.

'No problem Nicky then?'

'Not just that seaside Noreen? Even Calais like? Get back Sunday morning you reckon?'

'Paris Nicky. Got to be Paris. Because now you come to mention it you got the chance to do something wonderful.'

'Eh?' Something wonderful meant something I never wanted to do. 'Now I come to mention what Noreen? I only just thought about it myself. Come to mention what?'

'We go up Paris have a nice romantic weekend Nicky.'

'Yeah . . . '

'Only we get the chance to take someone else who never get a holiday. Who never got the abilities to take themselves — '

'Jimmy Foley?'

'Mrs Shillingford.'

Oh my good Gawd.

'Oh my good Gawd,' I went.

'Ain't that a lovely idea?'

'Well Noreen — '

'Help some old lady, some old lady you been ever so kind to Nicky so she reckons you're like her grandson and her star man and the cream on her cake . . . ?'

'Noreen — '

'So that's sorted then Nicky innit?'

★ ★ ★

Never any point arguing with that Noreen. Never any point arguing any woman, once she got it in her bonce it never took any detours. Probably Noreen got it sorted already with Mrs Shillingford weeks back, all stitched up and only waiting for me to open my big gob so she could take the opportunity.

One thing you found out when you got grown up, women were a fucking sight cleverer than geezers.

So there was never a lot you could turn round and say. Noreen made the arrangements and we were going.

Only first off there were a couple errands back home. Then first of all there was call for a serious talking. Before we went I was wanting to clock what the fuck was going down here. You got wasted, only fair you knew the reason why.

Invited George my warrant officer and fucking TT Holdsworth and Jimmy and Rameez and that little Bridget Tansley and Elvis and Paulette. There was a whole lot more going down than I knew about and it needed brain. Then again there was a fucking sight more the fucking Old Bill could turn round and tell us when they felt like getting their dongers out.

★   ★   ★

We met by Mrs Shillingford on Greenleaf Road just up from Walthamstow nick. Reckoned we could give her a bit of a party and do some business simultaneous. Never wanted to meet round my gaff nor get clocked together in public so we met by Mrs Shillingford.

'TT,' I went. 'Now you fucking going to turn round and tell us who whacked that Oliver Mannion or what?'

'Nicky we are following several lines of inquiries. As soon as we make an arrest we will announce it. Meanwhile we have a number of leads but have drawn no firm conclusions yet.'

Everyone laughed the fuck out of him. Budgie for his bosses. Bridget Tansley clocked a story straight off, even the fucking *Walthamstow Guardian* spotted a lying copper. George got out a chuckle. The rest howled. Mrs Shillingford seemed likely she might do herself a mischief. She never heard a lot going on, she never clocked a lot out of her beadies only she could tell a lying copper just off his vibes.

'Them others up the Tamil gaff,' I goes. 'They was never treading on my toes. No way was they. They was after that Diana Mannion innit?'

TT clocked me thoughtful. 'You reckon Nicky?' he turned round and said. 'You reckon they were after her? Why was that then?'

'What the fuck you askin' me for?' I went. 'You supposed to be the fuckin' mastermind CID here TT, you want to tell us what the fuck going down here, know what I mean?

First you put her on my case on account of you reckon I can blow someone away — '

'I never sent her Nicky — '

'Then they all start trying to whack her soon as she comes round our manor. Got to be a warning stay clear, then she never does so they warn her a bit heavy. Only problem was just when they were doing the bit of work there was some other geezers in their face. Someone trying to break my legs for me innit? Got in their face.'

'Yeah Nicky right on,' they all went except Old Bill and that Bridget. 'Yes Nicky right on,' goes Mrs Shillingford, bit later than the rest like an echo. She was getting in the groove now Mrs Shillingford.

'Got in the road, finished up Whipps Cross on the police protection. More overtime for the bleedin' filth.'

'Yeah,' they all went. 'Know what I mean?'

'Lads,' goes TT Holdsworth, yacking to us familiar like they do after they went on a course. 'Lads you have a serious point here. It does seem that there might be two parties of villains associated in this affair.'

'No!'

'Fucking leave it out TT,' I goes, 'you got to be a fucking genius no danger. Only ain't there one other small bit you trying to be avoiding here, you hear what I'm saying?

Only one other serious point like who you reckon whacked that Oliver Mannion?'

'Nicky we are following — '

We all howled again.

'TT,' George turned round and said, 'I weren't a warrant officer thirty years for nothing. Some of these kids they may look a bit stupid — that matter some of them are bleeding stupid — but one or two of them got a bit of brain. Might be best you told them everything or nothing. Otherwise they only guess for themselves. And you want their help, ain't that the case?'

TT did some thinking. Eyebrows job. 'Can I trust you lads?' he goes.

Plaster nearly came off Mrs Shillingford's walls. We hooted and hollered. Best time I had in plenty years laughing the fuck out of Old Bill. The fuck they taught them these days?

'TT,' George turned round and went again, 'you got to know anything you say here is round this borough in twenty minutes. If that's what you want then say it. You want to keep it shtum though it's best you button it. Not all bad lads these, no way. On the other hand you trust them?' He cackled. 'Excepting Noreen and Mrs Shillingford,' he adds hasty. Then he cackled more.

'Mr Marshall,' goes Mrs Shillingford, 'you

have wisdom in your ears.'

'Er, yeah,' he goes.

And that little Bridget she was scribbling and scratching like there was no tomorrow. When it broke she got it all down there, no problem.

One thing now we reckoned for sure. Old Bill got a touch on who whacked Oliver Mannion. They got a touch only some reason they never followed it up yet, preferred Diana did it for them. Then in the bargain someone was after sorting her game out.

Complicated matters.

Mickey Cousins was after slapping me up. No connection Oliver Mannion. Old problems bore a grudge.

Mickey's boys got in the path on some other geezer's boys. So his boys finished up Whipps Cross. Next question was if they got in the same ward Diana Mannion got in.

We went up for finding out. Before we went up Paris.

★ ★ ★

Finding your tracks round Whipps Cross was harder than getting Not Guilty up Magistrates' Court. We shanked up and down and round a few circles till we got the ward.

Guess what there was Old Bill patting down the customers. Guarding their property.

Jimmy was there had an interest. Me in the bargain. Rameez was there brought Aftab for company. We never wanted more, bring attention.

Old Bill always brought two on protection. Never one never three. They posted their two outside the ward, check the punters early. Same as usual though one of them was off for a smoke.

No need for a tactics talk. Never a chance like this again. Never such an oppo for mashing up some boxers.

Rameez and Aftab gave a diversion. Rameez never truly wanted being any diversion, wanted in there getting his carver out doing a bit of the old artwork. He had to grant it though it was me and Jimmy suffered the agg, got the debt owing. So he did us a favour the one time.

Two sharp Asian geezers never had to do a lot for making Old Bill suspicious. Walk down the street too quick and get done on a stop and search. Here up Whipps Cross they walked past the ward a couple times, clocked in the lobby, clocked Old Bill then showed themselves started running.

Asian geezers running got to be major villainy. Old Bill started running after them.

Old Bill yacking into his radio while he was running.

When he was gone we shuffled in that ward me and Jimmy. Not a nurse in sight as usual. Three boxers down one side, one two three. One sitting next up his bed getting over his spot of concussion. One face down on account of he got shot up the arse. Other one still unconscious.

Jimmy walked up the geezer recovering concussion. 'All right mate?' he went.

'Wha'?' went the geezer. 'Whe'?'

'No problem geezer,' Jimmy went. Picked up the geezer's flower vase and smashed it all over his bonce. Got a nice slice down the side his skull. Slowed down his recovery off that concussion. Water ran down red. Daffs stuck on his dressing gown, geezer looked definite worse for wear. Sounded none too clever either, started more of that moaning. Then Jimmy took that vase what was left of it and stuck it in the geezer's mitt, look like self-abuse.

One down two in the frame.

Geezer got shot up the arse was sleeping. Not a care in the world no bedclothes. In the bargain no hospital pyjamas only dressings on his bum, giving it the air if you please. We went over and tore off his dressings.

Arse looked like blotting paper. Blue white

and pockmarked. He woke up very sudden. By this time though we got our belts off and we gave that arse a fucking good whacking. One moment he howled and turned over exposing himself dirty bastard. Very soon turned back again when we whacked him there instead.

Screaming.

Not a lot of time left. We went over by the unconscious geezer tipped him up so he fell out still unconscious. Bonce hit the ground bump. We got our belts back on and we gave him a kicking. Nowhere round the danger zone for killing him, show a bit of mercy. Kidney damage maybe. One in the bollocks. Few in the gut. He stayed unconscious. We gave him about six each and left sharp. Blood coming out his hooter was a bit worrying. Still he was in the best place for getting mended.

Off down the corridor no problem John. Except find the fucking way out of there.

We already heard off Reception how they sent Diana down some private fucking hospital up the sticks round Goodmayes way. No time for that now, time to be small.

We were gone.

★　★　★

We needed finance. I got savings put away only we needed fresh finance for that trip up Froggie.

Mercedes Marty Fisherman owed me a favour so he lifted a few dinner sets out of BHS on Selborne Walk. Easiest piece of nicking round Walthamstow. Junkies doing it all the time only their problem was they never knew to do it without drawing attention. Junky lifted a dinner set so he went back an hour later and lifted another one. Taking liberties. Marty gave the bit of work some respect.

Arrangement was Marty got nicked and I paid his fines. No nickings and we shared the profits. It was like an investment. Anyhow Marty took time out from nicking motors, went in there and lifted a dinner set all in its box. Next day went back and lifted another. No problem so he went back again in the afternoon. Retailed them up the snooker hall in five minutes. Not a whole heap of dosh only cover a few vinos up Froggie.

Dean Longmore helped on a motor sale on account of he was an international these days. Nicked a French number up Kensington, smart item, Renault, Paris plates. Being as they were on holiday the Froggies got all their documents in the motor. Dean brought them over and I did the translating. Then he took the motor over Calais that night, sold it for francs off some geezer in a lock-up by the harbour never asked many questions. I got a quarter the profits. In francs.

Last off I got lucky. I got the word off Sherry McAllister who got the word off Ronnie Good. Bank robbery coming up on Hoe Street. Midland next to the Granada. All it was, I went down to watch. Only I got lucky.

★   ★   ★

We never got traditional bank raids up Walthamstow any more. Main problem was the exits.

Building societies you could forget it. All of them down the market and you got to be pissed even thinking on it. Run out the bank and fall over a load of breadfruit. Banks were more round Hoe Street. Granted you could drive a motor down Hoe Street only you ever clocked the traffic round that way and you understand the problem. No exit.

Only one left was a reasonable bet got to be the Midland. Still on Hoe Street but just before you got clear. Park the motor down a side street and all you got to deal with was fucking Sureways Parking. Out and away, head for Forest Road or up Church Hill. Or

98

carry on straight up Hoe Street past the Bell and hit the North Circular.

Securicor used to be best on bank jobs. Got plenty of advantages. Do it in fresh air on the pavement. Avoid distressing the fucking women and children in the bank. Avoid getting whacked in there in the bargain. Last but not least Securicor geezers always gave you the fucking dosh, not their problem.

Then it got awkward. They started putting that paint spray stashed away for surprising you. Open the fucking box and you got red paint top to toe. All over the fucking notes in the bargain. So you went up Kwiksave for your shopping after and you got a red coat and red hooter and red notes and they never turned round and said a dicky only outside the shop you got fucking Old Bill waiting.

I sat down by the bus stop over across Hoe Street waiting for the 97 up Leyton. Middle-aged biddie called Frances stood there, lived by Mum paid her rent on Church Hill and visiting her daughter up Beaumont Road. We settled down only a couple minutes and then the bit of work started.

Three motors out of Church Hill waited for the right-hand filter then pulled up sharp outside the Midland. All new motors nicked. One Ford one Audi one VW.

Two geezers out of each motor. Drivers

stayed in. One motor did a U-turn, came back and waited Church Hill. One went round the corner. Heard later he went down Greenleaf Road so he never minded the copshop was there and he never minded the speed bumps either. Last one pulled out blocked the traffic on Hoe Street so no fucker got in front and he was clear away.

Geezers got busy. All wearing stockings definitely old-fashioned. Three geezers with bats and the other three handguns. Bats for the doors, take care none got emergency locks. Made a good sound in the bargain. Guns for shooting.

They took the doors. Windows. Any bit of glass they went in swishing. And shouting. Plenty sounds. In case anyone never got the message they used the shooters a couple times.

Biddie Frances turned my way. 'Very noisy,' she went. 'Young people today.'

'True words,' I goes.

I timed them. Forty-five seconds. Good work. Coming out they carried full bags they took in empty. They got greedy though and carried some extra, never liked to leave any.

Running two each way swinging bats and waving shooters. Two over our way making Church Hill where the motor waited. One of them carrying his own two bags then dragging three extra bags he picked up. Cursing heavy. Dropped one in the street. Picked it up again. His mate shouting. He ran over. Dropped the fucker again by me and Frances.

'Fuck it,' he goes. 'Fuckin' fuck it.'

We stood still never liked to interfere.

'You fuckin' keep it Nicky,' he goes.

Nicky?

The fuck was he?

Bag sat by our feet. Geezer was away. Not a very big bag. Heavy though full of coins.

You never ought to lift coins off a bit of work. On the other hand coins they never got serial numbers. Even they sprayed them with paint you could wash it off.

Frances clocked me. 'You reckon those are pound coins in that bag?' she goes.

'Yeah reckon.'

'And how many you think there are?'

'Dunno Frances.'

'We could count them up later,' she goes.

Just then the 97 bus pulled up. When we got on it that cash was in Frances's shopping bag. We went round her daughter's and counted it and we got two hundred and fifty each.

7

On account of I gave up crime for Noreen we called in Wayne Sapsford and Mercedes Marty Fisherman for getting Mrs Shillingford up Waterloo. No way Mrs Shillingford got there without a taxi so little Wayne he lifted one. Took it off Lea Bridge Road when the cabbie stopped for a paper.

Wayne still reckoned he nicked a motor every day the week even now he was twenty-three. Never knew any other leisure pursuit. Reckoned he never nicked a London taxi before though. Made it a first. Grinning all day like a loon.

Best Noreen never knew the motor was nicked so we sent her up Waterloo first, make the arrangements. Best I never knew either so I got up there with her. Shelley Rosario came round for doing the woman bit with Mrs Shillingford, been in some taxis in her time. Wayne and Marty got Mrs Shillingford in the wheelie then carried it in the taxi. Shelley went in the back with her, Marty rode shotgun. They got up Waterloo like a beauty, never got stopped even one time. Mrs Shillingford never looked like any of their grannies either.

Noreen got the tickets together and apples and drinks and that. I hung out checking the French chicks. They looked me up like I was a cool dude.

Cab came in cruising, Mrs Shillingford sat up there like the Queen bleeding Mother, Shelley rabbiting on like Lady bloody Fergie only Mrs Shillingford never clocking a word she turned round and said.

'All right Nicky?' goes Wayne.

'All right Nicky?' goes Shelley.

'My man!' goes Marty.

'All right Wayne, Marty, Shelley?' I goes.

'Good day Nicky,' Mrs Shillingford turns round and says. 'I hope you have not lost Noreen anywhere.'

'Making herself busy Mrs Shillingford,' I shouted round her good side. 'Counting the cans of nutriment.'

'Does she have any mauby?'

'Put in a couple cans for you.'

'She a good girl. Where is the train? Did I tell you I have not been in a train since 1962?'

We got the wheelie out and went gentle up the checkin. Wayne and Marty and Shelley left the cab right there on the station, went home on the bleeding tube for safety. We were set.

Bit like a massage parlour that check-in up

Eurostar, big carpets dim lights and smart birds in uniform. Jesus they were a turn-on birds in uniform, never failed me.

Noreen had her little beadies tight on me though, make sure I never went under the counter with some little Marie-Claire. We went up the escalator got our seats in the chuffer. We were made up.

Last time I was down south was Ford prison round by Sussex. Better view out of Eurostar. Still sent me straight off snoozing though, never could handle that countryside, nobody there nothing happening.

Mrs Shillingford cream crackered by now, never could clock anything anyhow so she went off dreaming by Noreen.

Noreen reading about Froggie so she could tell us when we got up Calais. And she got a phrasebook.

'French for tunnel,' she went, 'did you know is *le tunnel*?'

'Leave it out Noreen,' I goes snoozing.

'And the French for vagina is *le vagin*.'

I opened one mince pie.

'Just checking you were asleep,' she turned round and said.

No one much around so I leaned over and put a finger up her vagina till she whacked me so I went back sleeping. 'Felt not bad for a Chingford bird,' I went mumbling. 'Might almost have reckoned you were liking that Noreen if you never whacked me.'

She was blushing like a mad woman by then though so she went off up the toilet all snooty after she propped Mrs Shillingford against the wall.

Then when I woke up again Noreen was changed into some French geezer in uniform talking some lingo I never heard before.

'Jesus!' I went.

'Ah Nicky,' goes Mrs Shillingford smiling smiling, 'you are awake. Let me introduce you to my new friend Hervé.'

'All right mate?' I goes.

'*Bonjour,*' he turned round and said. '*Enchanté.*'

'I reckoned you was Noreen,' I goes.

'She has gone for some coffees,' goes Mrs Shillingford.

'Coffees?'

'Hervé is from Martinique,' she goes beaming beaming.

Then Hervé goes into a talking up and down and round the bleeding mountains, fuck knows what he turned round and said only it was never French. Then Mrs Shillingford does the fucking same!

'Mrs Shillingford,' I went.

'Nicky yes.'

'The f . . . Er, what you speaking there?'

'I am speaking my own patois Nicky from Dominica. Hervé is speaking a cross between the patois of Martinique and the patois of St Lucia where his mother came from. He understands most of Dominican patois though and I understand most of him. He is a fine gentle young man I do believe.'

Old Hervé about sixty-odd, bit of a grandad only he seemed like he was plucking a few of her strings. She got a gleam in her mince pies Mrs Shillingford like she only got when I brought the fucking Bacardi out. Hervé doshed her his bleeding business card then he went off down the chuffer punching a few more tickets.

Mrs Shillingford smirking smirking.

★ ★ ★

Noreen already booked us some gaff opposite the station so Mrs Shillingford never had to toddle far. We got her wheelie out the chuffer only she reckoned she was wanting to feel the soil of Froggie under her plates. So we jacked it out the Gare du Nord and found the hotel across the square. Only took about a week and we were there.

'Evening lady all right?' I went to some old biddy behind the desk, forty-five if she was a day and looked it.

'Nicky,' goes Noreen, 'speak French to her you bleedin' idiot we only brought you here for that French talk.'

'You all right then mate?' goes the old biddy.

'Good evening young lady,' Mrs Shillingford turned round and said.

Turned out the madame spent three years down Plaistow married to some HGV merchant met her in some dock strike up Boulogne. Then when he drove off in the sunset she reckoned her best way making a crust was rip off the punters stepped out the Gare du Nord. So we checked in and wrote up our birthdays and life histories and everything else you got to do up Froggie. Then we went up our rooms. Not exactly the bleeding Ritz only better than home so we took a bit of time out. Mrs Shillingford got herself some kip. Noreen and I got a bit of nookie next door. What you do in Paris, bit of nookie.

Then we got a shower. Matter of fact we got one together. Then we went round Mrs Shillingford's room, woke her up and hauled her upright. Gave her a coffee we got from downstairs.

She settled. Put her specs on. Sipped that coffee.

'Mrs Shillingford,' went Noreen. 'Now you

tell us what you want most of all out of Paris. This is your holiday. We got tonight then tomorrow then we go back. What you want us to do?'

'Three things my dear,' goes Mrs Shillingford.

'Yeah right!' we go.

'First I want a nice French meal on the terrace.'

'December Mrs Shillingford,' I turned round and said. 'You heard it was December?'

'Shut it Nicky,' goes Noreen.

'Then I would like to drive in a sports car down the Champs Élysées.'

'Jesus.'

'Shut it Nicky.'

'Where we getting a bleedin' sports car?'

'Mrs Shillingford whatever you want.'

'You want me to borrow one or what?'

'Nicky you bleeding hire it of course. You go out there and hire a sports car, can't be too bleeding dear, only want it an hour. Don't you bleeding dare go borrowing no sports cars or any other motors no more.'

'Hire it what with?'

'Dosh you got plenty of Nicky I'm knowing that.'

'Only never no licence clever clogs, I ain't only never got no licence is all innit?'

108

Stopped her a bit. 'You ain't got a licence Nicky?'

'Ain't never had no licence.'

'So what was all that driving around you did in them stolen motors taken without consent? What was all that then, why it is you never got no licence?'

So bleeding straight that Noreen, you got to explain it from the start off.

'Disqualified Noreen innit? Never even let me get a licence, know what I mean? What I was always wanting natural, straight up legit licence. Only they disqualified me early doors, never even gave a feller a chance.'

'Like how early?'

'Like from birth Noreen. They never wanted me driving around. Conspiracy it was, hard luck story poor and unemployed, never give the working class a bleeding break, you hear what I'm saying?'

'Working class was about the only class you ever went into.' Never gave a monkey's for my hard luck story that Noreen.

'Went in French Noreen.'

'Yeah and much good it did you, get up Paris and what do you turn round and say only 'evening lady all right'? Useless you are.'

'Ain't never been up Paris Noreen. Maybe I never got the right accent. Anyway turned out she was a Plaistow bird.'

'Useless. What we going to do about this sports car?'

We sat there clocking round wondering what the fuck. We got to get Mrs Shillingford a sports motor. We never brought her this far for being disappointed. Noreen never did drive. We sat there giving it brain.

'Mrs Shillingford you got a licence?'

'No Nicky, I used to drive in Dominica when I was a girl but they never required a licence. I believe there were only three motor cars on the island.'

'I got to borrow one,' I went.

'Nicky you bleeding dare . . . '

'You got any other solutions?'

We sat there not yacking, not happy either. No other solutions. Jesus. There was never a choice, even Noreen saw that.

'Nicky you ever bleedin' take one back in England . . . '

'Mrs Shillingford,' I goes, 'what was that other wish then like?' That last wish? Get pissed up? Rob some Froggie bank?

'Oh my other wish is more private Nicky,' she goes. 'I think I shall keep it to myself for now.'

Noreen and me we clocked each other.

Then we went down for that meal on the terrace. Fortunate being December they got a terrace with glass round it. We noshed up omelettes and salad and I spoke Froggie, gave Noreen a right turn keep her romantic. Nothing like a bit of Froggie make you supercool keep the birds damp.

★ ★ ★

Early Sunday morning I was on the street. Only one solution got to be. Old-style Escort convertible.

Never had to be damage done, Noreen's conditions. So no break-ins no hot-wiring no smashed steering column.

We never wanted to be too fucking visible either so no fucking Merc job.

Got to be some crap motor still a sports car make you think you're a smart prick, then again such an easy entry you do it with the bunch of keys you brought out of England. As it goes I did bring a bunch of keys.

Got to be an old style Escort convertible. Ford takeaway.

Half-hour looking then I found one down some quiet street where they never woke up yet. All the streets round Paris they got flats and combination doors and concierges like they got in the blocks round Walthamstow now. Maybe they copied them off us. Got to be somewhere quiet then. Other side the Gare de l'Est by some canal was just the spot and a nice little Escort. Sitting there waiting for me, result time. Got a bump on one side only you clocked down the street and every other motor in Paris got a bump on one side, maybe they made them that way. Opened up nice and easy and we were cruising.

Except they put the fucking steering wheel the wrong side, course. I opened up the door on the right side forgetting then found they got nothing there. No problem though, minor adjustment to the plan and we were away.

Picked up Mrs Shillingford back at the hotel, and Noreen having kittens keeping her bonce down in the back.

Got to take Noreen with us though, not just me and Mrs Shillingford. Birds got their uses and one of them was they always could read a fucking map.

'Which way?' I turned round and said.

'Eh?'

'Which way we go?'

'Jesus Nicky you mean to say you don't know?'

'How the fuck I'm suppose to know? Never been Paris before innit? Serious man.'

She sucked on her molars and got her guidebook out her bag. Ten minutes we were there.

Noreen got us down the biggest square you

ever clocked, Place de la Concorde and that, all the fucking traffic going the wrong way round it. Then she pointed out which way the bleeding Champs got to. Then we were on it. Evil.

'Oh my,' goes Mrs Shillingford.

I put the roof back. Then we drove very very slow up the Champs clocking the fucking Arc. Only us going very very slow in Paris, rest of the geezers shafting each other up every traffic light.

Wind blowing round Mrs Shillingford's perm.

'Wow,' goes Noreen.

'Heavy duty,' I turned round and said. 'Big road, know what I mean?'

Mrs Shillingford got a massive grin round her chops and a kind of shine coming out of both cataracts. 'Oh my,' she turned round and said.

So we cruised around till I started feeling just a touch awkward. There we were, white boy, black bird and an old black biddy cruising round in an open-top early Sunday in December. They used to that?

We cruised off. Dropped the ladies back at their hotel then I replaced the motor where I found it. Or somewhere near. Parking space went by then course. Left twenty francs on the seat for petrol, Noreen's idea. Just so they knew for sure it got borrowed, I told her. She turned round and said mind my business, put the twenty francs there. So I did. Locked up again and scarpered right quick.

Then we went back to bed for another bit of kip before breakfast.

★ ★ ★

Paris was a bad influence that Noreen.

Rained all that afternoon so Mrs Shillingford snoozed on her bed clocking the TV. Reckoned she got the starters on that French language off her patois. Sound drowned out any noises off our room so Noreen got some easy reason for starting up again.

Sunday afternoon was Sunday afternoon you ought to credit. Couple of shots of the old vin rouge, geezer worked hard all week and wants to drop off in front the football. Never made difference it was Paris or Walthamstow. Only Noreen reckoned she got her juices flowing again, reckoned I got to satisfy her. Some birds took a lot of satisfying.

Then we winched Mrs Shillingford up again and we went downstairs for some more of that omelettes and salad and vino. Got Mrs Shillingford back upstairs for eight o'clock, she reckoned she'd take in some more of that

TV and drown the house out. Noreen was off taking me back down the old Champs.

More like the business. She wanted a drink and a movie, set me back half my giro only it was supercool. Fucking ace that Paris. We toddled back up our gaff happy as Larry, only blot on the horizon was I knew Noreen was after doing it again soon as we hit the duvet.

I was out for the count before I rolled over. Stuffed.

Two hours later I woke up hearing sounds.

'Noreen wh' 'appen?' I goes.

'Uh?'

'What them sounds? They coming from us?'

'Uh . . . ' She woke up a bit, pricked up, clocking.

Then she went, 'Nicky, you come over here now you don't worry about that.'

'Noreen . . . '

'You come here and give me a little cuddle . . . yeah . . . yeah you do that . . . '

'Noreen . . . '

Then she was moving all around and over. Sometimes when she did it she was like giving every bit of her to me. Moved like she loved me. Jesus.

Next morning we were getting a coffee downstairs me and Noreen. Just buying

another one for taking up to Mrs Shillingford. Geezer went past down the corridor and
out. Geezer in uniform.

'Noreen . . . ' I went.

'Yes Nicky?'

'Noreen you take a butcher's . . . geezer
went past there. You reckon it that Hervé off
that train or what?'

'Wouldn't know Nicky no concern of
mine.' Keeping her hooter right down in her
croissant. 'Here Nicky you don't keep staring
like that, you got that coffee and you all
packed up and ready to go or what?'

'Straight up Noreen I'm telling you.'

'One of them grand cafés for Mrs
Shillingford Nicky don't be forgetting.'

When we took her coffee up her room
Mrs Shillingford already got herself up and
about.

And smirking.

'You already up Mrs Shillingford?' I turned
round and shouted like normal for her.

'Hush Nicky dear,' she goes. 'My hearing
seems a lot better this morning, I don't know
why but I can hear you quite clearly.'

'Good on yer Mrs Shillingford. Want me to
give you a hand get in your chair for that
coffee?'

'Do you know I think I can manage my
dear. My arthritis seems a little easier also.'

Then she and that Noreen gave each other the viz. Little mince pies flashing, women only business. Then Mrs Shillingford sat there grinning and sipping her coffee and gazing out in space like she owned it.

8

She was writing away that Diana. Grunting
and moaning and writing away on account of
she never could talk. Always tough when you
got your jaw bust.

She got a fucking great writing pad and she
was filling it up right quick. 'I have suspicions
about the family,' she wrote down.

'What family?' I goes. Hoped she never
meant the Mafia. I started writing it all down
in the bargain till I remembered it was never
her lugs stopped working, only the vocals got
a problem.

'Oliver's family,' she went writing.

'You got family on your side?'

She stared over me, mist clouding up her
big beadies. She leaned over so I clocked her
tits down the nightdress. She gave a sob
adding to grunting and moaning. 'I have no
family,' she wrote slow.

'Mum and Dad split up? Yeah like a bummer
that, he get sent down or what? Never did no
good to a geezer and his bird, him getting sent
down. Want to take that into account I'm
telling you when they whack you a sentence
for doing some little bit of work . . . '

She took the pad and wrote very small. 'It was the mutiny . . . '

'Mutiny?' I turned round and said. 'I heard of that. Indian mutiny?'

She dabbed up her hankie. No more paper words. She gawped round the walls, out the window, in her Lucozade bottle, the whole bleeding shipping parade. Then she started on the pen again. 'I have suspicions about the family.'

Going to be a slow fucking job this it looked like. Then she put 'his brother Bernard'.

'Yeah.'

'His brother Rupert.'

'Rupert.'

'His sister Caravella.'

'Rupert. This Rupert geezer a black geezer?'

Pen and paper. 'No. Don't be stupid.'

I never knew a white geezer name of Rupert. Not so bad on a black geezer, fucking silly name on a white geezer.

'His brother Rupert done what?'

'His brother Rupert and his brother Bernard and his sister Caravella.'

'They done what?'

'I want them watched.'

'Any special reason?'

'I think they are after Oliver's money. My money.'

Now we were talking.

I shifted round put my chair behind her shoulder. Not so much on account of the planning chat, more I got a better look down her tits. Pity the jaw machinery got in the view. Only now we were talking. Least I was talking she was writing. It was news time.

'Them two brothers and one sister? They after his dosh you reckon?'

'I have no doubt. They hate me. They want to exclude me.'

'So they got you a slapping, put the message over? Or give you the permanent?'

'They always wanted to deter me. From Oliver. From being part. Now from finding out.'

'Lady,' I goes gentle considerate. 'You reckon they whacked your Oliver? You reckon it was them made his skull look like it went through the mixer? You reckon they sorted their big brother or what?'

Caused some proper wobbling round the jaw area some reason. Then she pulled herself up straight. 'Good God!' she wrote. 'These are established people!'

'Oh yeah course I was forgetting.'

'They might be after his money. They are not unemployed murderers.'

'No course not.'

'They are very well connected.'

'What you say?'

'As you know.'

'Say again? They got the connections this family?' Jesus it was the Mafia after all.

'Of course you know of the Mannions. They have always been MPs. Always.'

'Long time.'

'Oliver and his brother Bernard you know have followed the family calling. Rupert will be ennobled. Caravella is a Westminster hostess.'

I clocked her bit of paper more. 'This ennobled,' I goes. 'How you get that?'

'For services,' she wrote.

Shelley Rosario was big on services and our Sharon sent round hostesses on the visiting massage. They never got ennobled though, least not as far as I heard. Had to be they were working the wrong manor, needed to get down that Westminster way.

Diana getting zonked again now, lids shutting up gradual. In the bargain nurses were turning up wanting to stick more tubes up her and down her. Before she nodded off she pointed me up her handbag. Always a good sign. Passed it her and she counted out a big one. Plenty of paper in there, only flicked me a few notes.

I was cool. Every day the week I got given a big one.

She was writing. 'Received from Mrs Diana Mannion,' it went. '£1,000 for expenses incurred.'

'Received from Mrs Diana Mannion,' I wrote back copied the style. Copy the signature she wanted. 'Thanks and that. Nicky Burkett Investigations.' Then signed up.

No special reason it being £1,000 looked like. You made up a handy round number.

'I shall want receipts,' she went on another sheet. 'Itemized. For tax.'

Tax. Fuck me. I paid that tax once. Got a day on the building and they stopped me 25 per cent reckoned I was self-employed. Cost me a tenner. I heard you got tax back after, never got that ten back.

'No problem,' I goes.

Then just when she started snoozing I started going and nurses putting tubes in, what occurred only a geezer walked in.

Not such a bad bit of work being filth on the door, spot of witness protection on overtime up some private hospital. Chat the nurses. Decent nosh. Opportunity for meeting with nobs. Probably get asked for illegal check-up on some geezer's previous, run him through the police computer for a backhander. Then never be there when some smart dude wandered in, come in for visiting never mind he was welcome as a dose of pox.

Diana opened her lids one second and before I even clocked him she was wriggling shifting squirming like she sudden got bedsores all over.

Tall thin black-haired geezer. Long conk little gob. Looked like that Oliver except the back of his bonce was still attached.

'Diana my dear,' he goes.

Now her mince pies open wide and she was shitless at the geezer. Got to be she hated him or she fucking terrified. Or both. He gave me that creepy feeling. Like you got worms.

Nurses gave him the farewells, told him clear out while they tubed up. Fussed on Diana never liked him a bit.

'To wait for you my dear,' he goes to the nurses, 'will be the greatest of small pleasures.'

'Jesus,' one goes when he went out the door, kind of bleedin' customer you put up with in these frigging private hospitals. 'Now you,' she goes to me, 'you move yourself too if you know what's good for you.'

Diana still wriggling wanting her writing pad. Nurse gave it to her. Strong legs that nurse. No fat.

'Rupert,' wrote Diana.

'Rupert,' I goes.

'Rupert,' she goes again.

Visitor was Rupert.

He got to be checking her. Only explanation a geezer turned round and talked like him. He got to be biding, checking her runnings.

Might solve the first problem for the watching. I got out the door after him and made busy on the mobile.

★ ★ ★

Mickey Cousins used Tweedledum and Tweedledummer till they got in their accident. Then he got himself some boxers. Last of all he got to try security.

They were sat in a Merc outside the hospital.

Still a matter of finding out who slapped Diana and what the cause was. No special brain needed to reckon what Mickey wanted off me though. He wanted me hurting. All on account of we pushed him around one time he earned it.

Time used to be when security was ordinary geezers out of nick, only Uncle Bob you got was security. Wandered round some building site nighttime or made up the numbers on the M1 extension, get paid pushing poor fucking protestors out of trees. Now they reckoned security meant bouncers in the bargain. Shiny steroid geezers, bounce you around. Big geezers got a serious attitude.

They got to be from Mickey on account of the Merc. Likely two or three Mercs as it goes, stitched together after a few totals on the M25, bonnet off one, middle off another and the boot stuck on the back.

There I was waiting for following Rupert. There they were waiting for flattening my hooter up. It was very inconvenient. Two black geezers two white geezers. Four big geezers.

I hated big geezers.

I went back down the corridors trying the doors to the ops. Only a couple up the private gaffs. Got in one outside door, went up the next only you could clock through the window they were doing a fucking brain transplant. Or maybe it was toenail removal, all you clocked was it was one end or the other. Red alert anyway outside the door so I came back out the corridor. Next one I struck lucky. Got in the door. What I was after was some fucking surgeon's knife.

No ops due in this one it looked like and no one liming around. Then what did I spot only a little beauty, lying all nice and handy in some silver tray. Never needed the tray. Put the knife comfy in my pocket.

Then got the fuck out.

Jimmy Foley came by the main entrance in some gleaming stonking black Golf. It stood there shaking. I belled Jimmy before I clocked security out there waiting for me. Came in handy now though.

Jimmy turned the Golf round. I stepped out and stepped past it. Right up the Merc standing there all silent. Buried the scalpel in their front tyre before they got out the motor. Yonked it out again hissing. Switched very swift up Jimmy's Golf.

'The fuck out of here!' I screamed.

We were gone.

Chucked the blade out the window further down. Two miles later remembered we were following Rupert. Fuck it. I got a few calmers off Jimmy and steadied down. One thing about Jimmy he always got a supply in his pocket, never knew they might come in handy.

★ ★ ★

Past the football fields by the railway line I took Noreen behind St James' Park. Cold wet day coming up before Christmas, only a few days to go. Wanted to show her something so we took a Sunday walk.

Some kid got behind the fence some time.

There on some water marker he wrote his poem.

> I love Tanya and
> That's how it stays
> Because she won't break it off
> Because she loves the sex
> And I love her
> So I won't break it off.

Noreen giggled and held on my arm. 'You reckon?' she went.

'Kid got it sorted.'

'Dream on Nicky,' she turned round and said. 'Dream on Nicky.'

'True to life innit?' I goes. 'Geezer loves his bird pure, only she just wants a touch of howsyourfather, know what I'm saying?'

'Dream on.' She had a wander round swinging her little legs. Came back. 'You reckon I only stay with you for the nookie?'

She gave me the look.

Gave me the shakings all over.

'Nah nah Noreen,' I turned round and said very hasty. 'Only joking Noreen you knows that, just a geezer's little laugh and that.'

'Better believe it Nicky.'

She put her mitt in mine.

Then she put it down inside my belt.

'All the same mind,' she turned round and

said, 'be a bit disappointing if you never got nothing down there mister . . . '

We both went cackling like Geordies and running all the way over that field.

9

'Tiefing Magpies!' cried Slip. 'Tiefing magpies dey is! Only tiefed my Cat D is what they did I telling you!'

'Why they did that Slip?'

'Took a little stroll Saturday night and they is holding it against me! Even when I have only the best little cricket pitch in the whole wide world no exception!'

Visiting Slip up Highpoint, my old cellmate now he got transferred up country. Out in the sticks with the fucking sheep up Suffolk.

'Four apples two bananas six peanuts three teas two coffees!' he goes. 'I is on the health jag now I due for release Nicky! Only I not getting that exercise and fresh air now I confined to barracks! It one scan-dal. And I lose twenty-eight days adding insult to injury!'

Slip got in the open wing up Highpoint, gave him his Cat D on account of they found out he made cricket pitches. They got their cricket field there so they made him chief guard dog.

Jimmy Foley went for the canteen. Jimmy took me up Highpoint in a Renault. 'So you back in the Main now Slip?'

'Back in the Main like you can see Nicky since you is sitting here in it now. Back as a Main man. And all since that chief number one governor he done believe I is taking a stroll Saturday night!'

'Stroll down town?'

'Yeah I is taking the usual stroll you know Nicky out the prison and down that town seeing as Cat D got no fences. All natural normal like a man does Saturday you is knowing. Got me they pizza and chips up town Haverhill you understand — '

'Haverhill like seven miles off?'

'Haverhill like seven miles off I telling you Nicky a nice stroll, get me pizza and chips and maybe one little pint or two, make me way back up this pri-son, no problem bothering anyone then what do I find only I is on governor's reports Monday . . . '

'Nah.'

'Yes man I telling you! And governor believed it! Believed I take a stroll! I who is making his cricket pitch lovely lovely! It hard, it bounce, it take speed it take spin and all they batsmen love it too, it the best little pitch in the whole England in fact it the best little pitch in the whole world outside Jamaica! Me roll, me water, me roll again, me cut, me talk to it nice, it a beauty . . . '

'Governor's pitch eh and he turned round and believed them lies — '

'Well not exactly lies Nicky you dig on account of I did take that little stroll but you don' expect the man believe that when just four fuckin' screws is reckoning they saw me and I do that cricket wicket for that governor what he play on with his team when my team from Cat D we can spare it . . . '

'No fuckin' justice Slip, never any fuckin' justice . . . '

'Nah.'

Jimmy came back with the grub off the WVS. 'Fuckin' poxy tealeafing cows,' he goes. 'They only fuckin' rumped me on the fuckin' change again them fuckin' cows.' Only geezer in England you could count on having a ruck with the WVS was Jimmy.

'Only Slip,' I turned round and said.

'Yes my man?'

'Ain't it the truth they play that cricket in summer? Only now being December, you hear what I'm saying? Christmas coming up?'

'Hardly the point Nicky, hardly the fuckin' point. Trouble with you man always was you ain't got no aesthetic sensibilities, not one at all. Cannot appreciate never mind whether they actual play on this cricket pitch this minute, you dig? If they is wanting to play on it, it ready. Understand? Never mind it Christmas or Easter or you fuckin' birthday. You got that aesthetic sensibilities?'

'I ain't got none of them for definite. Get them up Suffolk or what?'

'A-E-S-T-H-E-T-I-C . . . ' he wrote it down. 'For certain Nicky you got to get some of them before you is going up Senegal innit? Treat the brothers sensible and that?'

Oh my Gawd. When we got in that cell together up Wandsworth Slip always had that notion we were headed for Senegal.

'Senegal!' he goes now. 'We make that import export! We take them little computers we take them designer clothing we sell them up the brothers and sisters in Senegal where my grannie's grannie she came from!'

Oh my Gawd.

'And you is speaking the language Nicky my brother!' Just on account of I spoke a bit of Froggie.

'Slip,' I goes, distracting the conversation like, 'now you back in the Main here, what the quality?'

'Quality shit. Quality I telling you shit. Quantity plenty you got weed you smoke out your arsehole you want. Problem is, you feel like the brown you got that enough for making a fuckin' sandwich also. I sorry to see so many brothers on that gear truly I telling

132

you Nicky. They on the gear serious man shooting up the works not only smoking. Serious problem man.'

'On account of them tests?'

'All on account of them tests bro'. You take the little weed, now they got them tests in prison it show up twenty-eight days after. So you get a positive and you lose them little fourteen days' remission. Then you take that her-o-in, that show up only three four days in they tests. So what they do the brothers? They take the brown course! Yes please one little ten-pound joey sir! And all they brothers get hooked man, not taking that little weed lovely lovely no more, only taking that gear then getting hooked and owe ten-pound what is more, and where they get that ten-pound man eh?'

'So they get in debt.'

'So they get in debt so they get mash up and you got gang war on the wing you dig? So they go down the block get away from they creditors, then they got four days clucking, get the sweats and no sleep and they hallucinations, problem.'

'Problem.'

'Problem.'

'You tried that soap Slip?'

'I did heard about it.' He cackled stuffing bananas and Twix down his gob, spluttered then cackled. 'I heard you is eating half a bar soap then the weed never shows up on that test, that right?'

'Right.'

We all cackled. 'Reckon I rather fail that test,' he goes. 'Reckon I rather fail that test man ain't that the truth?'

We were up for giving Slip his Christmas present and get the fucking way out of London. He never had long to go now Slip. Even when he got governor's and lost his Cat D he was still coming up release after Christmas. He was one contented geezer now. He was planning.

'You is seeing Nicky,' he turned round and said, 'that potential we got up Senegal, that capitalist entrepreneur tiefing business potential we is having along they brothers and sisters innit?'

'Slip,' I goes.

'Yeah Nicky my bro'? Yeah you is saying?'

'I got one or two questions.'

'Shoot away. Shoot away they questions. You is wanting to enquire about exports, licences, them little legal tricks what we don' fuck around with anyhow?'

'Nah. One or two other questions.'

'Yeah! Ask them questions!'

'You remember I went to Jamaica for you.'

'I is remembering, natural.'

'And we got couple of bits missing in the planning stage.'

'Planning was A1 Nicky. That planning was A1 business entrepreneur. Problem was operational man. Little bit operational fatigue syndrome was all the problem.'

'Oh that was problem.'

'That was problem.'

'So you give me the picture straight up on this one then eh?'

'Straight up my man!'

'What contacts you got Senegal? I turn up there and don't know no one, don't know nothing. Where you stay and how you get started on the business?'

'That the question? That all the question?'

'That the first question.'

'That the first question. No problem. No problem at all man. Next question?'

'Next question we know them computers and shit you take out Senegal. What the fuck you bring back?'

'Bring back? My man is saying bring back? They African products course Nicky! They African products!'

'Like?'

'Like . . . well you is knowing Nicky like . . . yam . . . '

'Yam?'

'Yam yeah course! Plenty plenty yam!'

'Yam in my suitcase or what?'

'Don' be fuckin' silly Nicky. Jesus man you ain't never had no real imagination your problem. Too heavy carry in your suitcase. You getting a container man!'

Stopped the conversation some bit that container. We sat back sipping our teas clocking Slip gobbing his apples. We clocked all the birds round the visiting area, some of them sitting the geezers' knees giving them erectors. Getting on for closing on visits now so all the weed and smack getting passed over, swallowed and that. Screws closing their beadies not forgetting they got their cut later. WVS in the bargain, probably smoking the confiscateds getting a rush. How it goes.

'Slip my man,' I turned round and said.

'Nicky my man!' Got his gob full. Never allowed taking any grub back off visits so he was gobbing it all speedy.

'Want to ask your advice geezer. Need a sensible geezer.'

''Bout fuckin' time! You is needing to ask my advice many times man but you too proud too stubborn too stupid too fas' man! Ask away! You fuckin' just ask away! Any special subject you want to ask my advice or only you life in general?'

'Knew you want to assist Slip. Only it about them capitalists. You reckon them

136

capitalists you always running on about?'

'Capitalists! Yeah I is knowing them capitalists like we is going to be you and me. Fuckin' real tiefing bastards innit?'

'I reckon I met some of them. See I got this bit of work on as it goes. Seems like these geezers they might be them capitalist bastards you turned round and talked about.'

'Ah,' he goes heavy.

'Hah,' he goes serious. Went to turn his chair round for the serious viz only they got nailed down. 'Give it to me Nicky,' he goes. 'Give me that whole scenario business plan fuckin' programme spreadsheet desktop window opportunity I want it! Now!'

So I gave him the knockings. Told him the SP on Diana and that Rupert and Bernard and Caravella. Gave him the scrip on what she wanted off me. Reckoned I needed a few words off someone brainy, some clever fucker and not too close. Seemed like Slip got to be the answer. He listened up.

I finished the tellings. 'They them capitalists?' I turned round and said. 'You reckon they them capitalists leeches bloodsuckers you always running on about in our cell?'

'They is them people. Nicky I telling you they is them people! They is them aristocratic imperialist entrepreneur-type bastards shoving they sweeps up chimneys and stitching they sweatshops all over the world! They is them people!'

'They the geezers you want us being in Senegal, right?'

'Nicky,' he goes sighing.

'Yeah?'

'Nicky.' He leans forward confidential. He beckons me closer. 'Nicky I telling you we is different.'

'Yeah?'

'We is brothers.'

'Brothers? Slip I got to tell you you ain't never succeeding in passing me off as no brother. Not that I ain't willing you understand me only I just ain't never got the skin colour innit?'

'You ain't got the cool neither Nicky.'

'FIVE MINUTES!' yelled up the chief screw. 'CAN YOU FINISH UP IN FIVE MINUTES PLEASE!'

'Nicky you got to understand we is ripping off the brothers in Senegal but we is doing it gentle. We is alternative rippers. We doing it one brother to another, keep them profits in the community, we is community entrepreneurs. Not like them free-market bloodsuck tiefing capitalist pinstripe vipers name of Rupert!'

'So what we do Slip?' Get him back to ground level before he took off. 'Woman made me an offer. How you reckon I handle it?'

'Rump them my bro'. Like them WVS did to friend Jimmy here. You got to have a modus operandi like I been telling you before. Your modus operandi is, you rump them. First you take their folding money and you do their little duties. You overcharge them like all good entrepreneurs, you understand? Then you put the cash with a little bank manager. Then you rump them round the block, rump them on the street, round the corners — '

''Scuse me Slip before we go out here. How we do that rumping you reckon?'

'Well Nicky you got the experience.'

'Ah no. Got me enough of that experience.'

'You got the experience, easy peasy Nicky you just stab you a few. No problem Nicky know what I mean?'

Jimmy gave him the gaze. Not often Jimmy got a surprise on account of not often Jimmy listened. Jimmy gazed this time.

'Slip,' I went.

'Yes Nicky?'

'I gonna ignore that. Only before we fuck off you tell me one more thing on account of you got the knowledge.'

'I got the knowledge true.'

'That Diana she reckoned I just got to

watch them geezers. She reckon they never bopped their bro'. They just after the dosh now he dead. So I watch them like see them conspire.'

Slip he gave a cackle, kind of pitying.

'What you reckon? You reckon they smacked him?'

'Nicky let us get one thing straight here. They all the same they people. They after the dosh. He dead. Ergo they smacked him innit?'

'What that word?'

'What word?'

'Ergy?'

'Ergo Nicky. One of them capitalist words. Ergo they teach you on them corresponding courses. You not bother with it. Just concentrate on them not smacking you in the bargain my friend. They not gentle people I telling you.'

'They smacked him.'

'They smacked him.'

Simple. Pretty fucking obvious matter of fact.

⋆ ⋆ ⋆

We passed him his weed for Christmas me and Jimmy then we were out of there and down the car park.

'Nicky.' Jimmy went slow.

'Jimmy.'

'I always wondered Nicky. You reckon your mate there he got any vital part missing?'

'What you saying Jimmy?'

'Like he got his motor in right enough, he got enough revs for a Merc. Then again he got his rad, he got his cooler, he got the pistons, fact he got too many pistons . . . '

'Yeah?'

'Only problem is he ain't got no fuckin' steering wheel Nicky, you hear what I'm saying?'

I cackled. 'Hear what you're saying Jimmy. Nor no fuckin' speedo either, know what I mean?'

'Nor no fuckin' thermostat. Nor no fuckin' indicators.'

We got in that Renault Jimmy lifted then we went cackling back to London. Then we took the motor back. Since we went up Paris I got a thing about taking motors back. So now I got Jimmy leaving the Renault just round the corner where we borrowed it. Maybe they reckoned they forgot where they parked it. Had to be that rehabilitation. Leave the fucker just where you lifted it then run like fuck on account of the whole world clocked you. Made sense to someone probably.

Diana was yacking kind of clenched. And sucking like the top off her pizza only not getting the crust. 'This is really a restaurant?' she went hissing.

She reckoned on account of it was a business meeting we got to meet in a restaurant. What you did.

'Well it ain't no snooker hall and it ain't no supermarket,' I goes. 'Reckon it got to be a restaurant. What you reckon Aftab?'

'Huh,' goes Aftab.

'Pizza Hut,' I turned round and said. 'Restaurant.'

'Fish,' goes Diana. Least it sounded like fish. She sucked on a kidney bean. 'What have you learned from your inquiries?'

'Took some advice,' I goes. 'Off my adviser.'

'What was the advice?'

'He reckoned I got to have a modus operandi.'

'Yes? And what form would that take?' Not fazed by my modus, never asking me what one of them was.

'He reckoned you was all them capitalists and be best I stabbed yous all before yous stabbed me.'

She was having a bit of bother with that

potato salad she got now. All round her gob. Better she got it liquidized.

'And what then?' she turned round and said. 'What would we know then about the people who murdered my husband? How far would you have investigated this mystery?'

'Oh yeah that. Reckoned you just wanted a sorting. Forgot you wanted a solution. We got one of them too though no problem.'

'Mystery,' goes Aftab. 'Solution.' Geezer of words Aftab.

'Who is this man?' goes Diana.

'Aftab.'

'Yes I know that. Why is he here?'

'Minder. Case your mates wanting for busting your mush again like.'

'And this one here?'

'That Rameez. He here case we want a psycho.'

We were there for reporting. Not only we visited Slip for the brain work, Diana gave us an address in Chelsea where that Bernard lived. She reckoned she wanted him followed might provide the answers, see what he was plotting up. We followed him. Now we got the news.

First off was a problem though on account of none of us knew where the fuck Chelsea was. Then Aftab got it on the A–Z. We clocked Bernard by his home. Looked like

Rupert. Looked like Oliver excepting the back of his skull.

'Lady,' I goes. 'We been following him.'

'Yes?'

'Aftab and Afzal, you ain't met Afzal, they the ones been following Bernard. Followed him up that Parliament ain't that the score Aftab?'

'Uh Nicky. Score.'

'Yes?'

We ate our bits.

'Yes?' she goes again. 'And?'

'Yeah,' goes Aftab.

'Turn round and tell her Aftab mate.'

'Monday,' Aftab turned round and said. 'Went up Parliament. Went home midnight. Chelsea.'

Fucking coleslaw was too creamy. Getting up Diana's hooter.

'Tuesday,' Aftab carries on. 'Went up Parliament. Went home midnight. Chelsea.'

'His mistress is in Chelsea,' goes Diana. 'His constituency is in Shropshire with his wife. When Parliament is in session he lives with his mistress in Chelsea.'

'Wednesday,' goes Aftab. 'Went up Parliament. Went home midnight. Chelsea.'

Thursday today.

'Sound like a fuckin' murderer to me,' I went. I made up my mind. Only fair give her

144

the opinion. Now was the time. She never liked it she still doshed. Investigation was non-refundable. 'We reckon they kept it in the family,' I went.

Diana she put down her fork and she looked at me.

Long pause. Bit of watering. 'You think that is the case?' she goes.

'All think so. Me plus Rameez plus Aftab plus my consultant. All think so.'

'You are an intelligent man I have no doubt.'

'Some doubt about that lady. Carry on.'

'But I cannot agree. At least I must retain some doubt.'

'No problem know what I mean?'

'These are MPs. These are comfortably off people. They are of course after his money but I cannot believe they took his life.'

'Bopped him lady.'

She blubbed. She waited. She mopped up. She spoke in between the chokes. 'At the least we must have proof if we are going to come to these conclusions.'

'Need your help on that one.'

'I must help you.'

'Give an assist.'

'Together we must find out if they are after his money. Together we must find out who murdered him.'

'Nicky that sound like two cases,' goes Rameez. 'Two investigations you hear that. Two packs expenses innit?'

'Sit here long enough missis,' I turned round and said, 'and you find out for sure who smacked him. Come round smack us in the bargain. Find the answer only not very good tactic. They following us for sure.'

'I feel so safe with you and your friends,' she goes. 'I have been so frightened. Rameez though is very reassuring, such a very dear boy.'

'He a psycho innit Rameez?'

'Sometimes in life, Nicky, we have need of a good psycho. Rameez may be such a man.'

'Oh.' I sat there a bit gobsmacked. 'Follow your thinking.'

'And what were your other plans?'

'Oh . . . yeah. Other plans.'

'Tell her Nicky,' goes Rameez.

'Well, yeah.' I got back in the groove. 'Well, see we reckoned we got to take positive action like my consultant went. Shit on them before they shit on us you understand. Like that Bernard.'

'Yes?'

'You wanting to find the score. So either we blackmail the fucker get the pics him and his bird. Or we lean on him heavy. Beat it out of him. Or that Rupert be a pleasure. Rameez and Aftab and Afzal whack him up a bit. Pain threshold situation. All it cost you their petrol money and a drink. Couple of notes. Valuable time you understand only they do a professional bit of work no messing around.'

She leaned over pointed her fork. Clock down her tits again when she leaned over. Vinegar dripping off the beetroot. 'What exactly are their hourly rates?' she goes. 'The British workman should be paid a proper wage for doing a proper job. I have not yet had an itemized list of expenses from you.'

Jesus. Bleeding paperwork again. I got to get Noreen on that, woman's work. And we got other understandings to sort out here on the payments.

'Hourly rates?' goes Rameez, spelled out the problem for me. 'The fuck she on about Nicky?'

'Lady Diana,' I goes, 'you got to understand them hourly rates is a thing of the past. Aftab and Afzal and Rameez is self-employed. Get paid by the bit of work. Piece work. Take performance motors now you're talking three big ones. Take one little piece of protection fifty notes. Twenty microwaves out a warehouse, one K. None of them hourly you get my meaning?'

'I think so . . . '

'Then again you work on expenses and it never fuck up your dole money innit? You start getting paid proper and they want your fucking P45 you hear what I'm saying? Noreen never let me work foreigners anyhow, reckon it illegal. Expenses though no problem. Least that how I sees it, not run it by Noreen yet granted.'

She clocked us.

'Like one of them tax fiddles,' I goes helpful. 'That make it easier?'

'Ah,' she turned round and said. 'Ah now I understand.'

'Yeah?'

'Of course. You see we always put the whole of Oliver's political affairs down against expenses. As you know a parliamentary income is insignificant and the real money is made outside. Parliament does have its consolations but — and I would never have told Oliver this — it can be really a tiresome business for a meagre income. There are also some very odd people in Parliament these days you know. Even in the Tory Party I'm sorry to say.'

'Yeah right,' goes Rameez, never cared who the fuck was in Parliament.

Only now Diana was wound up, food going all ways still couldn't open her gob proper. 'And in case you need financial advice,' she went, 'I know a good man, a little man in Berkhamsted we have used for years.'

'Bear that in mind,' I went.

Only now we were thinking on how long we got. All of us getting restless except Diana, been sitting there too long in the open and wondering when Mickey Cousins or MPs or whoever the fuck it was came along. Needed to be getting the business settled and make our moves.

'Miss Diana,' I went. 'Sake of example you say it never was the family banjo'd your Oliver. Say he got more problems up there, them Lib Dems and that? Or the family and them Lib Dems all in some stitch-up? You reckon there some way finding more on all that? Get in that family and do a bit of stir-fry?'

More pause. 'I have been thinking,' she went. Accounted for the pause. 'I have been thinking for some time.' She sipped on her coffee, get that in the jaws no messing. 'I wish to invite you Nicky.'

'Yeah?'

'I wish to invite you to the New Year party.'

'Yeah?'

'It has always been a family affair but most of Oliver's associates from the house will be there also. It is part of the season for the parliamentary ski club.'

We all clocked everyone.

'Ski?' goes Rameez.

'Ski?' I goes.

Aftab grunted.

'Where that?' I asked.

'I want to introduce you very discreetly to the occasion. I am convinced something will come to the surface because so many will be there and they must talk. Or take documents there. This is what I am hiring you for Nicky. I want you to see them all together, burgle their rooms, run through their papers, their chequebooks, find out whom they are sleeping with, perhaps assault one or two — the usual sort of thing.'

I never turned round and said a lot.

'You should arrive on the thirtieth. I shall get my girl to arrange everything. Then we shall play it by ear when we see who is there and where they are staying.'

' 'Scuse me,' I goes eventual.

'Yes?'

'That party like. It out the borough?'

'Pardon?'

'Don't reckon that ski club meet in Walthamstow. They go up that ski slope up Ally Pally or what?'

'Don't be tedious Nicholas, you must know where the DHO meets for New Year. Vengen of course.'

'Vengen?' I asks.
'Vengen?' goes Rameez.
'Vengen. In Switzerland.'
'Ah,' I goes.
'Ah,' goes Rameez.
'Huh,' goes Aftab.

★　★　★

Put Diana in a cab take her back Hertfordshire. Walked down the cab rank by the Central.

'I loved him,' she goes.

'Don't take it hard,' I turned round and said.

'He had a difficult life. Sometimes people do not realize how difficult it is for the comfortably off.'

'Know how you feel.'

'They all had it hard. Their father was absent for much of the time. Their mother was an alcoholic.'

'That why their eyes all too close together?'

'Oliver was the one who turned out well, who was loved by everyone. Yet he worried you know. He took the cares of the world on his shoulders.'

'Heavy.'

'They were taught that money is everything. But it is not you know. With even a small private income one can get by quite satisfactorily.'

'True words.'

'In spite of everything I loved him. I am empty now.'

We walked on a bit. 'Only one solution innit then lady?' I goes.

'What is that?'

'Fuckin' get the bastards eh?'

She gave it thinking. 'That would certainly help I will confess to you.'

Put her in the taxi still leaking. 'And be careful of Rupert,' she went. 'He is a demon.'

Right.

10

'Switzerland?' goes Noreen. 'Switzerland?'

'Yeah. Switzerland she turned round and said.'

Noreen stood there.

'That somewhere round Sweden?' I goes.

'Nicky you reckon you're going up Switzerland all on your tod you got second thoughts coming mister.'

'Be fair Noreen, her idea innit? Not my plan of action, know what I mean?'

'And all them Swiss maids? You dream on Nicky.'

'Noreen . . . '

'All that yoghurt and yodelling? Bound to get your juices going my friend. I heard all about that Switzerland I'm telling you, Nicky you ain't got no chance so you just get it in that little brain here and now, you understand me?'

'Noreen she reckoned only some family New Year drink-up, never mentioned no Swiss maids yoghurt and that.'

'Nicky take it from me, Switzerland is full of them Swiss maids. Chocker. And they're all fit birds I'm telling you. Blond-haired blue eyes and fit and all yodelling like there's no tomorrow. You ain't going there on your tod mate not now not no time, don't even think about it.'

'Noreen . . . '

'All in favour of you doing a bit of work legal, you know that.'

'Noreen . . . '

'All in favour of you even sorting this woman's problems. Get paid, fair enough. Come off the dole. Pay tax.'

'Tax! Noreen it all on expenses . . . '

'Pull the other one Nicky it's got bells on. Pay tax. Do the bit of work. Just try not to kill anyone this one time is all. Get your wages come home again like working in a factory, just leave them dead people alive. Only you ain't going anywhere near them Swiss maids in all that snow and them St Bernards and all them cuckoo clocks — '

'Noreen . . . '

Bit of a long pause, then she started giggling. 'So only one solution Nicky ain't there?' she turned round and said.

'Yeah?'

'I got to go with you. Look after you. Stop you falling off them mountains. Help you stay out of stupidness.'

Oh my Gawd.

'Yeah?' I goes.

'Yeah. That all right with you?'

'Noreen . . .'

'Yeah?'

'Be cold up Switzerland. In the fucking Arctic innit?'

'Good so that all settled then. Take a few days' holiday and I come with you on this jump-up on New Year. Book the flights, the business, you do the bit of work and I does a spot of skiing.'

'Noreen that great! Friggin' result! Yeah!' Got to show a bit of enthusiasm. 'All kosher then Noreen. You get it sorted, them tickets and what have you. That Diana she reckons she book us in some hotel. Be like Clacton I reckon, all hotels. So we never give a toss where the fuckin' country is, get on a plane, get off again, there you fuckin' are, Switzerland.'

'It's past France Nicky case you want to know.'

'Yeah?'

'And before Italy.'

'They do pizzas?'

'Maybe.'

That was sorted then.

★　★　★

So next I went up the probation office for a spot of travel assistance. What you went there for so they reckoned, advice on your problems.

'Rosie,' I turned round and went up Reception. 'I came for some of that advice.'

'Oh yeah?' she goes not looking up. 'You had a brain transplant then or what? Thought you knew it all there was to know.'

'Rosie I'm serious here I'm telling you, want to get some advice off that Andy. He in?'

'You going to wish me good morning first Nicky or you too busy following the straight and narrow these days?'

'Oh yeah ... sorry and that Rosie. Morning.'

'Saw your mum up aerobics the other day. She reckoned you were a changed man Nicky, reckoned that Noreen got something the police and prisons and probation and social services never got between them.'

'No doubting that Rosie, she got something that Andy never got for sure. My mum up aerobics?'

'Yeah aerobics. She loves them steps Nicky you know that?'

'Jesus. In them tights and that?'

'In a leotard yes Nicky.'

'Jesus. Rosie that Andy in or what?'

'I'll find out if he can see you. He may be busy.'

'Never too busy to see me Rosie you know that. You spare some of that coffee you got there?'

She pushed her mug through the window while she got Andy on the blower. He came out bustling always bustling Andy. 'Nicky! Nice of you to drop in, something you never managed to do when it was a court order. How's business? Killed anyone lately?' Always bustling Andy. Always sarky in the bargain, marking my card.

'Andy good to clock you mate. Treat your sarcasm with the contempt it deserves. Andy mate I got to ask your advice. We go inside.'

'Suppose that means you want a coffee same as usual.'

'And a fag Andy you know that.' I gave up smoking years back except for weed only I was never going to turn one down off Andy. He never smoked only kept them for the punters.

'Not allowed in government buildings these days Nicky unless you're suffering severe stress and you might attack me if you don't get one. Health and safety regulations. Which is it Nicky or both?'

'Just give me the bleeding fag Andy and two sugars in the coffee. And none of that political bleeding coffee neither.'

'Come in and shut up for God's sake.' He

made with the kettle in his office.

He still got that bleeding left-wing coffee though. Drink a cup and kill some dictator.

'Jesus Christ Andy,' I goes. 'You offending my ulcer here mate. You not still got that Jamaican Blue Mountain coffee I gave you?'

'Might have slipped your memory Nicky but you gave me enough Blue Mountain coffee to fit in an eggspoon, remember? Good stuff I'll grant you but an eggspoon doesn't last many months.'

'Bring you another one next time I go over.'

'No thank you Nicky I prefer the official taxed article actually. Now what can I do for you? Rosie said you wanted some advice. She also said you must be taking the rise, is that right?'

'Advice on the world Andy.'

'The world? Is that all? Any special part of it or the whole thing?'

'Come to mention it, Switzerland. We going skiing there me and Noreen.'

'Good God Nicky.' He went total pale-faced.

'Pardon Andy?'

'So crime does pay after all. You think I can afford to go skiing in Switzerland? Have you got any idea what Switzerland is like?'

'None of that crime Andy. Noreen she got

an Uncle Bob like you know. Me I got a legit bit of work all expenses paid.'

'So what do they import from Switzerland? Magic mushrooms?'

'Andy you're digging me out here! When I ain't done nothing yet! No Andy I comes in here solely for advice, on account of you always popping off through that tunnel and I knows you likes a spot of skiing. Want some practicals here you reckon. Like what is it I'm wanting to take out them mountains? I need to nick them skis here in London beforehand or get them out there or what?'

'I'll ignore the crack about nicking the skis Nicky. Even you can't wind me up that easily. I suppose what you're meaning is, can you borrow them off me those skis?'

'And the gear Andy. Heard you wear a lot of gear for that skiing.'

Reckoned one moment Andy got a bladder problem likely to burst somewhere. He seemed cross. Then he made one big effort and got quiet and still. 'Nicky,' he goes confidential.

'Yeah Andy?'

'For your information you little toerag I don't possess any ski gear. And if I had a whole bloody sports shop I wouldn't lend it to you incidentally. What you do when you go skiing is you hire everything when you get out there. Hire Nicky. Not steal. Hire. It's all available, from skis to boots to jackets. Understand?'

'Oh yeah no problem Andy. No problem mate.' We sat there a bit, me puffing and sipping contented.

'Now Nicky,' he went, 'if there's nothing else I have to get on . . . '

'One other thing Andy.'

'Yes?'

'I did just wonder, me and Noreen like, what with me being on the dole and this travel like being good for the personality and that, if you . . . you know how you got that befriending fund dosh Andy what you used to give when I got in a crisis with my spends . . . '

Oh dear. Andy was cross. One moment I reckoned he was going to whack me on his filing cabinet. Him being nonviolent and all.

'Nicky . . . '

'Don't be fussing now Andy. Fully appreciate your problems mate, cutbacks and that. Only asking you wanted to make an exception one time, put a few bob the way of some poor bleeder trying to improve himself only fallen on hard times? You reckon?'

The time he calmed down was time for flying out Switzerland. Couldn't wait that long so I gave him the thanks for the advice and went out the door.

What I always turned round and said, what you never know yourself you got to know where you went up for the good advice like.

Noreen kneeling on the floor showing me her fanny when I got in that night. Big atlas spread out and map and guidebook. 'Nicky come here,' she went.

'Poke you through your legs you kneel like that.'

'Promises promises. Come here and look at this map.'

'That Switzerland?'

'That Switzerland.'

'Where that Sweden?'

'Some other bleeding map Nicky. Now look up Wengen in that atlas, in that index up the back.'

I did. I clocked it hard. I turned it round. It weren't there.

'I rang that Swiss tourist office Nicky. Got us some train tickets for Switzerland. Went to collect them in my lunch hour. You reckon where Wengen is?'

Followed her finger on the map. 'Nah,' I goes. 'Wrong name Noreen. We going the wrong place. That ain't Vengen that Wengen. W. For Willy. Wengen.'

'That the same place Nicky. They never got the hang of Vs and Ws them Swiss. That's

Vengen Wengen. How they say it.'

'Strewth. Gonna be fuckin' difficult Noreen, you reckon you up to this? Language problems. Hard enough for a geezer never mind some bird.'

Never failed. Wound her up like a clockwork toy. Time she finished battering me we were ready for bed.

'I got the plane tickets Nicky,' she went last thing. 'And the train tickets. We're all booked. You just got to fix up that hotel with Diana. All you got to do, the man's bit.'

'Oh yeah. Right.'

★ ★ ★

Christmas Eve I went round Kelly's on Aldriche Way for clocking the kid.

'All right Dad?' he goes when I went in.

'All right Danny?' I swung him round lifted him up. Big as a fucking boxer, like I was giving Mike Tyson a hug and a whirl and a kiss on the chops. 'You treating your mum good then taking her out for Christmas dinner or what?'

'We going round Nan's innit? You gonna be there Dad?'

'Yeah course.' Wished I never though. Shithead and Kelly all on one day, sooner do fourteen days down the block.

'What you got me for a present Dad? You got me a present?'

'Ooh, reckon I forgot about that. Get you a present next year, know what I mean?'

He cackled, knew better. Now Kelly came in the living room.

'All right Kelly?'

'All right Nicky?'

'Gestapo around?'

'Barry's out if that's what you mean.'

Kelly was fucking a German name of Barry. She gave me the Dear John for a German name of Barry. Say no more.

Matter of fact that Barry was an all right geezer for a Kraut. Went drinking with him one time got rat-arsed, end of the night he reckoned England deserved all the World Cups Germany won, I reckoned Germany deserved all the wars. Never let Kelly know though, keep her tingling.

'Where you taking Danny tonight?'

'Where you want to go Danny? Some rave-up?'

'Yeah! One of them drug places you told me Dad!'

'Best we get down Howard Road then. Every gaff on that street a drug dealer. Shoot-outs every night. Knife fights you name it.'

'Yeah!'

'You got your coat?'

'Yeah.'

'See you later Kelly.'

'See you later Nicky.'

We were gone.

Danny got on fair with that Noreen. That matter Kelly got on fair with Noreen, spent their time yacking about me and not comparing good points neither. My mum got on famous with Noreen. Kelly got on with Shithead, far as anyone could.

All meant the geezer with the attitude problem got to be me. They reckoned.

So now Danny came round mine for his Christmas Eve dinner. Made him bean stew.

First time I ever ate bean stew was round our teacher Marigold's when we were kids. So hot it was Wayne Sapsford shit all over her floor. I waited till I got home, shit all over Mum's floor instead. Now I reckoned on giving Danny bean stew, keeping that Kelly busy over Christmas.

Only joking maybe.

Danny loved his beans.

We got kidney beans and pinto beans and black-eyed peas and white beans and speckled beans and fucking rainbow-coloured beans. Plenty garlic six cloves. Onions, tomatoes, heap of chilli and couple of carrots. Molasses. Pepper. Salt. Danny cooked it up with me, all I did beforehand was soak the beans a month or two. Piled them all in, lit the match and Roberta's your bleeding uncle.

Noreen came in from doing her last-minutes for Christmas. 'Smell that garlic coming out the tube station,' she went. 'Fact I reckon I smelled it up Oxford Circus before I went in the tube.'

'We making this ace fuckin' stew Noreen,' goes Danny.

'Danny,' I goes. 'You ain't only seven years old innit. Don't you dare use that kind of language, right? Till you at least eleven years old you turn round and you say bleedin' or friggin', right? Got that? No fuckin'?'

'Got it Dad. Noreen this friggin' stew's bleedin' ace, you hear what I'm saying?'

'Give me a taste?'

'No! You got to wait your turn!'

'I'm so hungry though I reckon I could eat a little boy boiled up in there so you want to watch your back.'

Danny beaming. 'We already put a big woman in there Noreen. Make it sweet Dad reckons. Got it in one of his recipe books.'

'Smart-arse.' She kissed him and went off for changing. Only trouble with that was I always made it tough keeping on cooking when Noreen went off changing and showering and that, never could get my brain off her taking off her undies. Got to be the garlic made you French. Still I concentrated on Danny and stayed in the kitchen.

'Dad you turned round and said put some wine in there?'

'Yeah why not. Splash of vino. Going foreign next week got to get used to it.'

'That when you go up Switzerland?'

'Yeah. In them mountains.'

'Dad,' he went. 'Me and Mum was talking.'

'All right son. Won't hold it against you.'

'She reckoned you got no chance up Switzerland. She reckoned you and them Switzerland people never understand each other. They speak English Dad or what?'

'Dunno mate. Speak Swiss I reckon. Noreen!'

'Yeah?'

'Danny want to know what they speak up Switzerland. They speak Swiss innit?'

'Some parts they speak French Nicky. Seeing as they're round by France.'

'That right? Got a result there then, give them Swiss maids a touch of my Froggie.'

'Only trouble is eighty per cent of the country speaks German Nicky. And that Wengen, that's in their eighty per cent. Don't understand French at all.'

Always was a bleeding know-all Noreen. Been reading the guidebooks on the quiet got to be. Never could put one past her.

We ate that stew up and Danny got four helpings then I took him back up Kelly's, told him to do his best.

Christmas Day never turned out quite how we expected.

11

Where they refurbished all up Priory Court Mum's block looked like fucking spaceship Mars Probe One now. We walked round from Howard Road Christmas dinnertime. We got traditions in our family. Tradition was at Christmas we gobbed our grub and gave the booze some welly and listened up Shithead eating sprouts and telling us things were never any good these days. Nighttime this year Noreen and me we were off round her mum and dad for a proper drink-up and some real nosh. Get the rum out for sure.

'So when was the last time you brought Noreen round then Nicky?' goes Mum. 'Don't hardly ever see you Noreen these days he never lets us together have a proper chat.'

'Nicky you give your mother all kinds of grief,' goes Shithead.

'Leave it out you jerk,' our Sharon turned round and said, giving her kid his grub.

'Hope he treats you better than he treated me Noreen,' Kelly put her oar in. 'Mind that Barry, now he treats a girl lovely and I won't hear different. Takes me up Charlie Chan's, bought me them slimming aids you name it.'

'Big news in Germany them slimming aids,' I went. 'No one weighs more than twenty stone innit. Hope he don't make you look like them Germans.'

'Nicky just because Barry's a German — '

'Kelly you mustn't rise to him,' goes Noreen. 'Nicky don't care if Barry's a German or an Eskimo, you know that. He's only winding you up.'

'Yeah, true words I suppose Noreen. He's a bleeder innit that Nicky?'

'Yeah he's a bleeder,' goes Noreen sitting next to me. Same time her little mitt creeping round my bum. 'I got to treat him strict, discipline him every day and that you know?'

'Nicky you want some more sprouts?' goes Mum.

'Dad you take me up Switzerland?' goes Danny.

'Too far Danny.'

'Too far mate. Past your bedtime when we got there.'

'Don't know what the world's coming to,' Shithead turned round and said. 'Never done an honest day's work in his life, now he's only going skiing up Switzerland. Some of us grafting away . . . '

'Nah Mrs Burkett,' Rameez went desperate. 'Tell you them sprouts was delicious only it against my religion to take seconds I'm telling you. And also Muslims we only supposed to be eating sprouts once a month maybe you never knew that?'

'Such a good boy that Rameez,' goes Mum. 'Good to his mum and dad, always polite, so religious . . . ' Mum never been in a church since she got christened.

'Nicky you been hearing on that deal round that cigarette load?' Rameez asked quiet. 'Driver in the deal, lift it there and then, whole container.'

'Rameez I'm clean these days you remember that?'

''Scuse me Nicky. 'Scuse my manners. I was forgetting.'

'Anyone want some more of that Lambrusco?' went Shithead. Then he stood up to lean over and pour.

Then he got shot.

Bleeding brilliant it was. That stage never knew who did it, never fucking cared. Maybe they aimed up Rameez only he just sat down. Maybe they reckoned Shithead was me, never a fucking compliment. Maybe Shithead got friends out there in the bargain, loved him like we loved him. Sitting in the block opposite in some empty flat it got to be some pro, never any kid with his airgun. Never a sawnoff neither, too accurate. Had to be a pro. Only trouble was they still never got him in the business area. Took him in the left shoulder.

All the same he dropped the Lambrusco out his right mitt, went flying back smacked against the wall. More mess on the carpet and then he started dripping blood on it.

'Henry!' cried Mum.

'Danny get here!' cried Kelly, not so stupid after all, got over him. Sharon dragged her kid under the table. Everyone knowing straight off what happening. He got shot.

Best fucking Christmas I ever had. Only wished I did it myself.

We were all down the floor by now and Shithead started the moaning. Whole lot of us dialling Old Bill on our mobiles, they got six 999 calls all the same time. Sharon got the lights off. Mum blubbing. Shithead still moaning. Better than TV it was, beat the Christmas movie any time. Shithead got shot up.

No time to enjoy it proper though. I dropped out the back window.

Nipped round and ran over the block opposite. Never clocked any special window for a shooting. And he was out of there by now for certain.

He got two choices, up South Countess Road or down North Countess Road. He got to have wheels. I went for South Countess nearer the main road.

And a geezer was walking up there smart in a suit.

And got a little suitcase like.

Only geezers wearing suits up Priory Court were fucking bailiffs. I never heard tell of bailiffs working Christmas Day.

I stepped up beside him. Working geezer he never learned his trade, had to be away quicker than that. I strolled up.

'Happy days,' I goes.

'Excuse me?' Only a fucking foreigner he was.

'Nicky Burkett,' I goes. 'Pleased to meet you geezer.'

'Pardon?' He stopped one second.

'You done me a favour mate. Best bit of laugh I ever got come Christmas. Plugged my fucking stepdad. Reckoned the least I could do was give you the thanking.'

He walked on a bit slow.

'Course,' I went, 'always some chance you were never after Henry innit? Some chance you were after some other fucker up there?'

He clocked his case where the shooter was. All folded up neat now, screwed and bolted and put away, not very handy in a crisis. I never got too close on account of I heard hitmen could be a bit useful on other bits besides shooters. All the same he had to grant

172

it I was holding the advantage here.

Mainly I got the advantage with Rameez catching up the action now and how he got a machete in his mitt about four yards long and he was swishing it.

So now I made his space. 'You care to spill the words then geezer?' I went. 'Like on where you get the bit of work from then eh?'

'Excuse me?' he went.

'Or my man here he chop your head off?'

'I'm sorry I don't understand,' he turned round and said. 'I have just been visiting my auntie for my Christmas dinner.'

'Drop the fucking case Ratzo,' goes Rameez.

'No.'

Rameez chopped a slice off his ear. I hoped we got it right. I hoped he never came up Priory Court for Christmas dinner with his auntie.

'Drop the fucking case.'

He dropped the case.

'Now you tell us who paid you the mullah,' went Rameez.

'I don't know. It was a man in a restaurant. I don't know his name.'

Rameez took a slice off his other ear. You got to hand it to Rameez he was delicate with that machete. Not an easy bleeding thing to do taking a slice off with a machete. He was

173

clean as a whistle. Do the same with his satsumas later.

Geezer sobbed. Not much of a fucking hitman. Not supposed to sob.

'A man called Rupert.'

'Next I take off your nose,' goes Rameez. 'Or you give us the money.'

Geezer shook. 'All of it?' he goes. 'I do not have it here. I was paid only a deposit in advance you understand.'

'Wallet.'

He handed it. Rameez opened it out. Never wanted his cards. Never wanted his picture of his missis and kids. Took the folding. Gave it me for counting while he scratched the feller's cheek.

£987. He probably got some petrol and a bag of chips on the way down, accounted for the shortage. I put it in my pocket.

'You not too bad on the aim,' goes Rameez. 'But you too fuckin' slow for a shooter. You ought to be out of here long past.'

'I know,' went the geezer blubbing some more.

'Since we got us some compensation now for the distress caused,' Rameez turned round and said, 'you better fuck off innit mate?'

He fucked off. Left a trail of gravy in the street and we heard an Audi start up and go.

We walked back up the Court. We left the

case there laying in the road, never touched it. We left two slices of lug there beside it for Old Bill to do their thinking on. Put forensics in a happy mood last a week. We got back in the building just when the sirens started.

Old Bill came in six motors. Surprised they had six available Christmas Day. Ambulances behind, three of them. All screamed in the Court.

'You got the pudding Mum?' I went.

Shithead still moaning.

'Anyone want to pull a cracker?' went Sharon.

'Rameez you be a good boy and pull them curtains,' Mum turned round and said. 'Keep them bullets out eh?'

'Rameez you got a blade for peeling them satsumas?' I goes. Knowing full well he threw it as far as he could down the gardens up Winns Avenue before the law arrived.

Everyone cackling now excepting Shithead, never did have a sense of humour. By the time Old Bill came in it was a right party.

Shithead went off to Whipps Cross and Christmas was never so bad after all.

* * *

Then before we set out we got to have one last talking. All a bit confusing so what it was,

I got to have it sorted in my mind so we made a plan of action before the trip.

One last talking meant all the boys.

Jimmy Foley and Wayne and Dean and Rameez. Elvis and Paulette. Shelley Rosario. Sharon came over. Bridget Tansley off the paper. George my warrant make it respectable. Even Andy my probation for the travel news. Noreen now. I was never pleased on Noreen being there preferred her safe at home, only Noreen got what Noreen wanted. Fucking TT Holdsworth made it his business being there. We met down Jimmy's caff on Markhouse Road, take in some Thai nosh on account of Jimmy's missis was Thai. Best café in Walthamstow no problem.

So we sat there eating our noodles and we got the facts out. We talked it round.

Me and Noreen were going up Switzerland. Diana wanting us there finding for sure who whacked her hub. And why.

Reckoned we already knew who whacked her hub. Bernard and Rupert and Caravella whacked her hub. Slip reckoned it and Slip was right.

Looked at from that point of view this investigation was kind of easy peasy. Take in a bit of skiing, spot of yodelling then tell Diana all the knockings. Collect the dosh. Only got to have a talking now for finding out everyone was the same thinking. And what about the complications, what they reckon on that?

And what we did if it turned awkward.

'Nicky you ain't got no problem!' goes Jimmy. 'You knows who did the whacking you takes the dosh!'

'Yeah!'

'You takes that bagful of exes!' goes Rameez. 'You gives the good news. You sort out the complications! Then you fucks off right quick innit!'

'Nicky,' goes Elvis, snappy thinker sees the problem. 'You always get the worries too much man. What you worrying now is why it all so easy, ain't that the truth?'

'Mention it Elvis yeah. Why it so easy? What the fuckin' problem here? And you be telling me one more thing, why it is them pigs never trouble arresting no fucker? You got the answers on that one?'

We all turned round and clocked TT. Been awful quiet since we got in there. One more serious thing I was wanting a talking for.

'TT?' goes George, been bothering him a while now in the bargain.

TT never turned round and said a dicky. He got him some more tea. 'Jimmy!' he called out.

Very confusing for Jimmy Foley got the same name like the guvnor of the gaff. He reckoned they got to be related. Now he just started up for getting TT his tea when he clocked the problem and sat down again.

'TT?' goes George again. Always the straight goer George, never liked a curved copper. He came round yours on the warrants did George, you paid a bit of your fines and he never nicked you. Never paid your fines at all he still got you another chance. Straight goer. Took his holidays up Clacton. Probably collected a few fines up there while he was stopping.

'I am not available for comment,' goes TT.

Everyone howled.

'And pretty fucking obvious the reason he never available for comment innit?' I turned round and said.

'Yeah?'

'It came clear to me just now and here, right? Sitting here clocking that TT it came clear to me. Like a fucking vision.'

'Tell it Nicky!' goes Elvis and Paulette.

'How he never wanted that whacking solved, know what I mean?'

'Nicky,' goes George, 'now you're getting in serious water here mate — '

'Tell it bro'! Right!'

'Well, it got to be he took a dip innit?'

'He took a dip? He got big pockets?'

'He got a consideration?'

'It got to be that. Either that or' — I was thinking faster than I was gabbing, or the other way round — 'either that or he got a PI in there giving him bigger news. One or the fucking other. Got a PI, never wanted to pull him out maybe.'

'He got a grass!'

'Either one of them two or . . . or he got the fear of nicking the big boys . . . '

'Yeah them big boys up Parliament, he got the fear!'

'Either one of them or . . . or . . . ' I went slow. 'Or he wanting me to whack them, simple. Keep it on the hush, you hear what I'm saying?'

They all went quiet.

'What I reckoned first time out when he sent that Oliver up my gaff. Got a consideration for sending him my way, sort out his problem. Now he never can get out the problem. In the bargain they never want a fuss round the big boys, never want any noise round them Members up Parliament. Then again maybe they reckon I wander in there provoke a bit of evidence like. Then what it is, maybe they got a PI. Ah fuck it, fucked if I know. TT, you want to tell it then fucker?' I was more confused than when I wasn't confused.

'Nicky . . . ' goes TT. It went real quiet

again. Little Bridget scribbling scribbling. 'Nicky . . . I could never consider . . . I could never consider getting you or anyone else to kill our suspects and solve all our political problems on the quiet . . . without any public fuss . . . surely you know that Nicky . . . it would not be ethical or in the interests of justice . . . '

Then he upped real slow and went out the door.

Then it stayed real quiet even longer. Till George reckoned he better turn round and say something important.

'Well . . . ' went George.

'Well mate . . . '

'Well . . . ' went George again.

'George mister you reckon you got a bent copper there or what?' went Rameez.

'Not bent,' went George. 'Not bent not TT. I better not say anything. I will say though I think he might be under a bit of pressure somewhere. I think he just tried to tell you that.'

'Ah,' went Jimmy, still never understood it rightly. Trying though.

'Ah Jimmy,' went Elvis. And we all reckoned we got the basic knockings now. All we needed to know anyhow and fuck the rest.

'Nicky,' went Noreen, 'only you got to remember one thing now. You never get a lot of support off the Old Bill you hear what I'm saying? You sort their problems out for them and they're sweet. Things turn awkward though and you find you're on your tod. And what is it you always start doing when it gets like that? You only start killing geezers innit? Always the same. And it ain't allowed now.'

'Noreen be fair!'

'Nicky,' goes Rameez, 'you want any shafting done you just put out an advert mate. You done your bit. Put the word out and we come running no problem. Help you out.'

'Not you nor none of your mates,' goes Noreen. 'None of that killing I'm telling you. Nor thieving nor robbing nor speeding nor . . . nor any of them other things you used to do.'

'Yeah course Noreen you got it.' Proper embarrassing everyone clocking how your bird ran your life. Supposed to be private. Noreen you got to say was some cantankerous bird.

We sat there and gave it thinking.

What we did know, TT sent Oliver to my gaff. Then he got whacked, not part of the plan.

Best TT found out who whacked him. And Mission Diana meant one way or another we could solve their problem. Either they cleared up after or they never needed to.

So he was cooperating with us and we were cooperating with him.

Nice to be of assistance to the fucking pigs.

And going to be interesting up Switzerland.

12

We got on that plane.

Noreen she packed her long johns. Then she packed her long johns for me in the bargain, reckoned I was only a short-arse could get in them easy. Sounded like a result to my way of thinking only then she reckoned not the same pair she was in, stupid. Then she packed up her woolly hats and gloves and shades. Enough sun cream make you turn out like a seal. Last off after her dresses and that she put in about a thousand pairs of knickers. Me I took two pairs of underpants case one got froze up.

Second plane I ever went on. Flew up, flew off, flew down again no problems. What they were supposed to do. Plane full of Swiss geezers. Never clocked any geezer yodelling though giving it that.

Then their fucking trains were something. Been on some trains in my time, mostly Walthamstow Central down Liverpool Street. One time I got a train back from Southend when I never found a motor for getting home. Even got that chuffer up Paris. One thing I never did though, I never got a train up a fucking mountain before.

First off they got a train in the airport, kind of handy. Noreen got the tickets already. We were headed for Interlaken first she reckoned. Fair enough. Got settled down all ready for a bit of snooze. Then she started out on the travel news.

She told me where we were headed. Where we were never headed. What they spoke and where they spoke it. How they fancied their breakfast. What shape their cheese got. How they turned round and said howdy. What you did with your skis when you wanted to piss. How many Swiss francs you got to the dozen. What a banker looked like. Whatever the fuck you wanted to know, Noreen never stopped the rabbit all the way. Old Swiss biddies sitting opposite reckoned she was a madwoman. Fortunate though none the biddies got out of order on Noreen or I had to whack them.

Interlaken turned up. We got off our train and down in the subway and Noreen knew where we were headed so we came up the right place. Hard to tell for starters though. All they got on that platform was like a brown box on wheels. Going up in the mountains.

And the snow.

Plenty. Sudden you realized they got plenty snow everywhere round there. Back home no snow at all.

And the fucking mountains.

I never realized they were there. Two small mountains lay off one side, nothing to write your grannie about. Then I looked up between them, and Christ. One line of big fuckers. Massive against their sky. One special one tumbling down. Jesus. You ski down that? Felt my bottle gone already.

Train went chugging across the valley then in the trees. Then beside some road we split up. Half the train went up some other valley on the left. Our half went up that valley with us in it.

Lauterbrunnen. Town called Lauterbrunnen. I was never likely ever forgetting that name.

Smaller than Walthamstow.

It was starting getting dark. Up ahead top of the mountains turned red. Even down our valley it froze.

All along the side of the valley they got massive mega cliffs like you never saw. Millions of feet up. Icicles ran halfway down them. In the town their station was dark like out of hell.

Snow on the street. Snow on the line. And another train, we got to climb off our train and cross over the tracks to get on it. Kind of primitive you ask me. We lugged our bags over, two tons of Noreen's knickers.

We climbed up the other train, kind of mountaineering practice. This one got wooden seats like a matchbox. And inside cheery geezers. I hated cheery geezers specially sixteen-year-old cheery Swiss geezers all singing and got skis. Least I reckoned they were skis, I never clocked one before but for definite they were too long for skateboards.

'Noreen where we going in this truck? Cold in here fucking freezing.'

'See them lights Nicky?'

'Yeah. Up there, yeah. So?'

'We going up there in this train. Them lights is the edge of Wengen.'

'Nah!'

I clocked up the mountain then back at Noreen. Never wanted to be taken for a melon. 'You're having a laugh innit Noreen? Be reasonable woman, this box of tricks up the fuckin' mountain?'

We went up. In their snow. Up the mountain. More fucking snow than you ever clocked in your tiny life. And winding up that hill we went backwards and forwards, sometimes facing the mountain sometimes looking back over the valley. Fucking smart you got to grant it, never born yesterday the Swiss geezers. Never even seemed like steep.

And then we were up Wengen.

* ★ *

'All right mate?' I goes to the geezer behind the desk.

'Good evening sir,' he turned round and said. 'Welcome to Wengen.'

'Thanks mate. And the same to you too no problem.'

'And welcome to Switzerland,' goes the bird by him, bit of a dolly, bits and bobs all in the right places.

'Thank you darling. Appreciate the feeling. Kind of clocks a nine out of ten from where I'm standing.'

She smiled at me like I was the jack in her box. She leaned over for getting the register, made me shiver all the way down to my little carburettor.

'Nicky you just go and sit over there now,' goes Noreen. 'I will attend to the registration for us both.'

Attend? Noreen was talking mean, hissing quiet like a shark. I went off round the gaff for a butcher's while she made with the paperwork.

Hotel was just by the station so you hardly even got snow on your boots when you came out. Hotel Silberhorn, just like that Diana turned round and said. Never looked that special from outside, kind of mouldy. Got

187

through the doors though and it was like walking into a warm pool. Deep carpet soft noise and everyone whispering.

'This is your first time in Switzerland sir?'

Jesus. Nearly made me jump out my banana. That damn dolly again, little dark-haired Heidi with knockers. Skin like a tub of honey. Noreen found me yacking to her and it was termination time, Bobbit job and no messing.

'Yeah you got it, first time and that. You do them guided tours then Heidi? Round them icicles?'

'No I am working mainly in the hotel. I am a student of metaphysics working here for the holidays you know?'

'Mega whatsit?'

'Metaphysics. It involves the study of what might be and what might not be, do you understand?'

'Oh yeah. Got you. What might be and . . . '

I could hear Noreen sucking her molars round the lobby.

''Scuse me Heidi catch you later only my missis need me urgent, got a serious grief problem here . . . '

'I will see you on New Year's Eve Nicky.'

She got my name already. Jesus I was a little charmer after all, got a touch here.

188

Good as gold Swiss people.

'Nicky!' went Noreen.

'Yes my darlin'?'

'Not so much of the darlings Nicky you save that for your little cowgirl friends.'

'You never minded that darling-ing last night Noreen.'

'That was different.'

'And William Tell behind that desk there he was fancying you like his cobblers were on fire.

She giggled. 'Leave it out Nicky.'

'I clocked you moving your bum like he was a bleedin' ace ski-jumping ice skating playboy millionaire banker no problem ain't that right?'

'Nicky we got to get up our suite.'

'Suite?'

'That Diana she booked us a suite.'

'Only some suite? We got to sleep on the settee? Or in one of the fuckin' armchairs? That the best she can fuckin' do?'

'Suite Nicky like we got three four rooms. Not suite like a three-piece. Suite like you go from one room to the other.'

'Eh?'

'All for us. Bedroom bathroom sitting room and, like, I don't know, coalshed maybe what have you.'

'Only us? Don't have to share?'

'Only us.'

'Jesus.'

Geezer waiting for showing us upstairs. Same geezer from behind the desk still got his mince pies on Noreen boring a hole through her. Smiling. Friendly geezer matter of fact. Too friendly. Back home last about five minutes on the estate.

He took us up the lift. Got out. Rolled out the carpet. There we were room 301. Suite 301.

Jesus.

He opened the door went in sniffed the air. Sniffed the front room sniffed the kitchen sniffed the bedroom. They all seemed like they passed the test. He grinned away happy.

'Welcome to Switzerland sir, madam. Please have a nice day.'

'You too mate.'

Passed us that key and slushed off. We were there.

Bags there already, bit of virtual reality got there before us. We stood still never moved. Never knew what to turn round and do.

Might still be there now only the dog and bone rang. Saved the fucking day.

It was Diana course. Checking us.

'Ah you have arrived. I hope everything is satisfactory.'

'Diamond so far lady. Diamond. Do some skiing right here.'

'We shall meet for dinner.'

'We shall?'

'Please come to my suite. Number 420. We shall eat here in the suite tonight. Seven-thirty for eight.'

'Pardon?'

'Seven-thirty for eight.'

'Oh yeah right. Catch you later then.'

She was gone. Bit of a puzzler.

'Noreen,' I went. 'Maybe some woman talk I dunno.'

'Yes Nicky, she troubling you? You want to tell me your pain?' She giggled.

'First off she reckons we eat round her suite. No problem.'

'Yeah.'

'Then she reckons seven-thirty for eight. The fuck she means? What time she want us, seven-thirty or eight you reckon?'

'Don't mean nothing to me Nicky, some ways they got. We just turn up seven-thirty, right, so no one get vex?'

Sounded like they got cooking round their suites, maybe make a cup of tea. We had a shufti. Tucked away in a corner they got a nice little cooker all mod cons. And a sink and a fridge. And a bar.

'Noreen!' I goes. 'You clock this? Got us

our own boozer here, you credit that? You want a vodka and orange or what? Pissed up before tea? Jesus Noreen we got lucky here. Then you cook us some little snacks any time I get peckish innit?'

'Dream on Nicky. Don't keep a man at home and bark yourself. Oh and Nicky maybe you want to check the prices on that bar.'

'Prices?'

'You got to pay mate. Vodka and orange set you back a fiver maybe. You check that list there?'

'Jesus. All in them Swiss francs not surprising I missed it. You reckon they translate it in real dosh?'

'We got them Swiss francs Nicky.'

'Oh yeah.' Only Noreen was in control here so we never got the drink-up. She reckoned we got to go on a healthy walk instead so we went on a little toddle up the High Street.

'Noreen,' I went on the way out the door, 'how much you reckon that suite cost then? Few sobs or what?'

'Best you don't even think about it Nicky or you start thieving again. Just say your two-week giro covers around half one night, you stay there sleeping till about four o'clock then they kick you out mate.'

'Jesus. You reckon that Diana she well lined or what then?'

'Just a bit Nicky.'

High Street was covered in snow. You reckoned up Switzerland they ought to just get their snow on the fucking mountains where they wanted it not all over the fucking pavement. Slippery as fuck. Then on the edge of town old biddies carried their messages or pulling some cart up the hills slipping and getting heart attacks and asthma the business. Least you reckon they might heat up the streets a bit, undersoil heating like the Arsenal. Maybe they never thought about it.

One end the High Street round the corner they got a Co-Op. Then they got a ski shop and across the street the gaff where you booked up for your skiing lessons. Then all round that square by the edge of town centre you got husky geezers and fit birds coming off their day skiing. Only some of them seemed to reckon it easier getting off the mountain on a sledge, dozens of sledges they got all round. Getting on the end of the afternoon and they all plodded knackered looking up their hotels. So wasted in fact hardly seemed worth the trouble, better off spending your holidays on Clacton beach.

Not in December granted.

We turned up the High Street for our little stroll trying on standing upright.

No motors in Wengen. Walk up the street.

Few little buggies run you down was all, no motors allowed it looked like.

Noreen put her little glove in mine all affectionate. Wanted to toddle up the main road hand in hand so all the world could clock you. Proper shaming. In the bargain all the punters were English or American not even foreigners, suss you right out straight off.

I never argued though not stupid. We toddled up there like she ordered.

They got mountain shops and tea shops and postcard shops and chemist shops. Restaurants mostly round the hotels. You walked down the road and on your right they got their skating rink. Outdoor skating rink all froze up. Other side the rink still a few skiers not doing a lot, skiing maybe.

'Nicky you want to buy me a hot drink for being so sweet?'

They got a special stall. Geezer never seemed to mind the cold, stood out all day. Grinning all over seemed very pleased to see us. Very pleased to take our hard-earned dosh no doubting. Leastways Noreen's hard-earned dosh.

'What you reckon he got for hot drinks Noreen? Horlicks? I ain't drinking none of that Oxo.'

'Good evening sir, madam. It is happy

hour. All the drinks are at half price. Come and taste them.'

'What you got mate?'

He got hot toddies or hot toddies. They got some other name in Swiss only we never fussed. We got two hot toddies. Turned out it was never like football matches, they got alcohol. Better.

Then Noreen gave the geezer a note and he never gave enough change to shake a stick at. Fact he gave her two coins so midgy you could hardly clock them.

Noreen carried it off like it was regular. Not letting some Swiss dude reckon we came out of Walthamstow.

Drinks though got you warm and randy.

We went up a clothes shop. Noreen she was after some Swiss undies, kind of a souvenir. Trying to finish me off I reckoned, sitting there like a big man while she yacked on with the damsel about teddies or whatever the fuck they got these days. I tried looking like a window model.

And we got a result there, no fucking teddies on the shelves. Maybe up in the mountains there they only wore polar bear skins. Noreen never liked to ask anyhow, pretended she was interested in their pile of ski pants.

One leg cost more than our flight over.

We went in one of their restaurants for grabbing a coffee. Rather Noreen grabbed the coffee. I got a tea. Then when I clocked the tea I grabbed the coffee.

Cup of tea came in a glass. Serious. 'Jesus Noreen,' I went. 'You seen my glass of tea?'

She started giggling. I put the milk in their tea and it went like cream paint. Then I put the sugar in sipped and it tasted like cream paint in the bargain.

They got to be sad people.

Never complained about the tea never want to hurt their feelings probably doing their best. Not their fucking fault they got a few things to learn. As it goes the coffee was ace. You just got to find out their ways.

Then we were nearly ready for the exit when I looked up across the room by the door.

Shit and fuck and bleeding fucking hell.

Villains were there.

Over in the corner was security.

Four big geezers in shades. The same four big geezers last waiting for me in a fucking Merc by Diana's hospital. Two big black geezers, two big white geezers. All big. All drinking tea out of glasses. Maybe they were cissies after all.

Mickey Cousins was here? Or I got it wrong and they were after Diana?

Oh fuck. Fucking fuck me.

They never clocked us yet. I shooed Noreen the other entrance and we went back up that hotel. Oh fucking dear. Serious serious aggravation.

13

Still you never wanted things to put you off your stroke. Get back in that hotel and you got to make best use the facilities. Happy hour got you in the mood with their toddies. Three rooms in their suite and we used them all. Noreen in such good form she near as bit my shoulder off. Altitude seemed to suit her.

Got in the shower and the jet knocked me over. Where Noreen bit me made me howl. Take a shower in Switzerland you got to be a hard man. Noreen took a bath. They put so many smellies in there she almost disappeared under the bubbles. Bits floating on top still looked all right though, couple of nipples.

Then when we went up Diana's she was all Miss Prissy like butter never melt in her mouth. Nor anything else you might think of.

Suite 420. Half past seven. We were feeling so mellow Noreen and me we went up there touching, moving slow, cackling quiet. We found 420 no problem.

The door was half open.

★　★　★

198

Everywhere quiet. All the punters sipping their cocktails somewhere or maybe only humping before supper. No one on the corridor. Diana's door open. Someone left in a hurry. It was never good news.

'Oh dear,' goes Noreen.

'Be careful Nicky,' she adds. Meaning it was me went in there first. Not a problem though. Door closed might be a problem, call in the cavalry. Door open meant they left. The theory anyhow.

I pushed it and went in. 'All right Diana lady?' I went loud just for precautions.

There was a noise and there was a rush. Someone leaving out the back.

Shit. Theory was no good.

They got another door in some of their suites, led to the next suite for company. Knew that now on account of that was where the geezer left by.

'Diana?' I went again loud. 'You all right girl? You in the bedroom getting dolled up or what?' Bleeding fucking obvious she never only there still might be some hard geezer knocking around. Give him his chances for escaping before I turned Noreen on him, mash him up. 'All right I come in then?' I goes. 'Seven-thirty for eight and that?'

No more noises.

I went in and after a bit I found her. Still in the bathroom.

Matter of fact still in the bath and kind of bedraggled. Water was deep and soapy. Diana got her bra and knickers on, not the normal way for taking a bath, least not round our way. Black bra and knickers. Bottle of Scotch nearly empty by the side. Pen and paper on the stool. I never bothered reading the note, some kind of stupidness. Fucking silly way for framing a suicide. Making it look you jumped off a bridge was one thing. Swiss bath was another no matter how deep they got them.

'Noreen!'

Came running.

'Which one of us you favour giving her the kiss?'

Bit of a pause.

'Go ahead Nicky you best do it.'

'Permission granted or what?'

'Only don't you go making a habit of it. Out on them ski slopes they don't need no kissing, they're all well alive I'm telling you.'

'She never looks good as you in the bath anyhow.'

'Thank you Nicky. Now just bleeding get on with it.' She was off running for the Alexander getting Reception hasty. I knew about as much on the kiss of life as about hang gliding. I heard you got to press on their chest though. And the kissing.

What with getting her jaw bust then her gob filled up with soap then me kissing her Diana was having a hard ride round the chops area.

I considered the problem. Not an easy job how to go about it on some bird in a bath.

Leaned over pulled her mush round, sort of hoicked her gob up and blew in. Yuck. Full of soap. All on my bleeding lips now. I could take that cannabis test and sail through clean as a fucking whistle.

Did it again blew in. No progress though not making any headway, never matching up the blowing and the pushing getting the air in her. I pushed down on her chest now, in out in out. Bit of dribble came out her gob not very impressive. I whacked her the kiss again, blew in, pushed on her tits . . .

'Yeeagh!'

'Nicky?'

'Got the fucking timing wrong I got a whole gobful soap and water there Noreen. Fuck it.'

Noreen got Reception on the blower telling them. I hauled Diana half out, there got to be a quicker way.

She weighed a fucking ton.

I tossed her over the side of the bath so her bum was in the air. She never looked so good from that angle. Lot of wobble. I smacked her on the back. Again. Pushed down on her. Sudden there was a whoosh! Big dollop of water and foam and spit and fuck knows what went all over the carpet. Clean it up, save them shampooing. Then a weird sound. That a moan? I smacked her again on the back pushing down again like a rhythm. Noreen standing by the door.

'Kind of get to like this, know what I mean?'

She clocked me like I was never worth waxing her vocals on. Got the don't-make-me-tired viz. You got to chuckle over that Noreen, bit of a classy bird no doubting. It killed me that look she gave, set me cackling there and then.

So there we were, me cackling astride over Diana, her half out the bath in her bra and knickers and puking up soap and water, Noreen giving it an attitude problem and none of us ready for cocktails just then, when three folk came in the door in their bibs.

Rupert.
Bernard.
Caravella.

Tall, thin, black-haired, long pointy hooters, mince pies too close together. Rupert and Bernard wearing the suits. Caravella wearing a little black number covered her ankles and covered her tits. Just. They stood there side by side. Then the staff came in behind them.

Our mate from this afternoon went off duty it looked like and Heidi along with him. Two new ones off Reception and the night manager and some nurse. They came running rushing making themselves very busy. Got yacking on the mobile and the internal and every other fucking thing. Then pulling and pounding Diana about. Piccadilly Circus in there.

Specially when the grub came in behind.

Diana ordered a meal for us from downstairs. Cook it there eat it here. Enough for the ambulance crew in the bargain it looked like. They came in just after.

Even fit in the filth if they wanted, Swiss Old Wilhelm after, geezers in uniforms straight out of the packet. Creases they could cut you with, save the energy on giving you the kicking. They stood about looking cute.

So in there we got Diana and the hotel staff and the ambulance geezers and the pigs and me and Noreen and then Rupert and Bernard and Caravella. Me covered in soap and water and a bit of gobbing. Diana in the bargain for that matter. All there eight o'clock on the dot.

Only they took Diana off for a pumping.

Then the filth started on the questions.

Main difference up there was they asked the questions kind of quiet. I was used to the full fucking shouting match. One of them was quiet on account of he never spoke English, kind of a dumbo.

'Fancy a spot of nosh?' I asked him. Clocked round the trolley, see what we got. 'Bit of spud and a cheese sarnie or what?'

'Good morning,' he turned round and said.

'Excuse me sir,' went the other geezer. 'The hotel manager he is telling me that you came in here just now because you were invited for the evening eating, that is so?'

'Yeah mate. Seven-thirty for eight she reckoned.'

He picked up Diana's note, manager already gave it to him. He shook his Judge Dread very weary like. Make allowances for foreigners he reckoned. Got their funny ways.

'It is very sad,' he goes.

'Tragic mate,' I goes.

'Very sad that anyone should think we would believe a note like this. We will make our inquiries. Meanwhile we trust that she will be satisfactory of course now in our hospital.'

'Right as rain mate I reckon, bit of the old stomach pump sort her out fit as a fucking fiddle, know what I mean?'

'It is fortunate that you arrived when you did.'

'Very fortunate just what I turned round and said to my bird here, very fortunate indeed. Saved her life innit? Reckon I get a Swiss medal or what?'

He never got very excited on that one. Instead he started on taking a few details off everyone.

'Nicky,' went Noreen very quiet.

'Yeah my darlin'?'

'That geezer who went out the other door when we came in.'

'Yeah?'

'It was that Bernard stood there.'

'Yeah?'

'Yeah.'

So it was Bernard MP reckoned he was going to give Diana the big drink in her tub. And now we were ready for having a spot of supper with Bernard and Rupert and Caravella. Very cosy.

Best we took a few precautions maybe.

''Scuse me guv,' I goes to the manager before he went off.

'Excuse me sir?'

'All right with you we still stay up here for eating up the grub?'

'Of course sir.'

'Them three over there and us two and the

grub and that? Just them three with the pointy hooters and Noreen and me for a couple of hours, you get my meaning?'

'Why yes sir. If you are liking we can send someone to call on you after one hour to see if you would like further refreshments.'

'Right fucking ace mate. Excuse my French.' So pleased I was I went forgetting my manners. ' 'Scuse me guv I was meaning to turn round and say that'll be just bleedin' brilliant. We just sit here have a quiet nosh with these bastards here, any sound of some hoo-ha and you come running know what I mean?'

'Of course sir. Any sound at all of some hoo-ha and we will naturally come running immediately. Now if you will excuse me . . . '

'Course mate. And good to have you around.'

We were left with the grub and three fuckers got their mince pies too close together.

14

Diana ordered us the Swiss nosh before she got in the bath. Turned out she wanted all the typical dishes like they got in the mountains.

They got to set it all out on bits of machinery.

They got a big pot on top of a candle. Least a gallon of cheese sauce in it. Gave us long forks and bits of brown bread. You dipped their bread in the sauce.

'Fondue,' went the waiter.

'Thanks mate,' I told him.

They got slices of baked potato and they laid them on little metal trays. You put bits of cheese on top the slices then you pushed them in a melter.

'Raclette,' went the waiter.

They brought sliced loaf and cheese out of silver paper wrappers. Already cooked up nice.

'Cheese on toast,' I went.

'Käseschnitte,' went the waiter.

They opened up a silver dish full of shredded-up fried potatoes with more of that cheese on top. They put a spoon in.

'Rosti,' they went.

'Rosti mit Käse,' went Noreen, clever clogs.

'Käse rosti,' they went.

'Fuckin' champion mate,' I goes.

They put bottles of Swiss wine on the table. Not a joke neither, Swiss wine. They poured it out case we never knew how.

They put a bottle of thick red stuff out. Some of it missing already. They reckoned it went in the cheese sauce, likely story.

'Kirsch,' went the waiter.

'Don't mind if I do. Fancy a half of that kirsch Noreen?'

'Just a small glass Nicky,' she went dainty. So I poured one out. They put some titchy glasses out for it hardly worth the mention so I tipped her glass of wine back in the bottle and filled it up with that kirsch. Then mine.

'Up yours mate,' I went to Caravella.

She and all of them they still never spoke.

The waiter went off with his boy. Noreen and me were left with the scum. Two scum geezers and a scum chick. Topped their brother. Nearly topped his missis. Gave me the heavy warning. Now we were dunking our brown bread in the cheese sauce together.

Fuck me.

'Pass the cutlery please,' Noreen turned round and said. She was getting slit-eyed was Noreen. She never liked these fuckers not one bit. She was never getting under the mistletoe with any of these on New Year's Eve. I reckoned she might do a bit of stabbing with that fork she got.

'Well this is nice,' went Caravella, first words she gabbed.

I got busy on the grub. And judging by that grub they got to be fucking strange geezers these Swiss.

Cheese sauce was A1. Fuck knows what they put in it and you got to mark it a bit unusual cheese sauce for your main dinner, only you got to give credit, it was major gear. I dipped and I dipped. Quick as I could on account of I never fancied it so much after that Bernard and Rupert got their bits in there, never appreciated their slobber on my chunk of bread. Caravella granted might be a different deck of cards, mix a few juices with her. I turned on their other dishes. Got some of their fried potatoes and cheese. Got some of their cheese on toast. Got some of their baked potatoes and cheese. All on the plate together though you had to admit there was something fucking strange about these Swiss. Not a lot of light relief it looked like.

They left a lettuce leaf out for each of us. I gobbed them all. Swished them down with the half of kirsch. Sweet as fuck so I got another half of white wine for a chaser. That was it. Fuck it. I finished my meal.

God.

Maybe I swallowed a bag of cement in there with the cheese sauce.

Stop all the Swiss geezers flying off their mountains in the wind maybe, hold them down tight.

For afters I swigged another half of that white wine and settled back. The rest of them coming near the end of their plates. So we finished the serious business, now we might be getting a bit of chat.

'All right mate?' I went to Bernard.

'Pardon me?'

'You done enough GBH for one night or you planning a bit more for later, know what I mean?'

'I'm sorry I don't know what you're talking about.'

'No course not. How about you Rupert mate? You got your heavies out here in the bargain trying for sorting me out? Or you only here for a touch of the old skiing?'

'I believe we may have met before,' he goes. 'Was it at the hospital? Were you there when my sister-in-law suffered her broken jaw? Perhaps you were delivering something to the hospital, the Lucozade or the medical supplies? I'm not quite sure how you gained access to the ward though. Or to Wengen, come to that.'

'Nicky,' goes Noreen.

'Yeah?'

'Hit him.'

That kirsch got to Noreen right quick. Made her violent. Needed counselling.

'Only you lady,' I went to Caravella. 'Not quite sure where you fit in the frame, you get my meaning? Bit of a high-class popsy, I heard you was a hostess. Meaning you do a bit of the old massage or you some MP's slag or what? I knows you got a tongue on account of it came out when you turned round and talked back then, so you knows how to use it on the punters that the case?'

I was maybe never making a lot of bosom pals there only I was kind of upset. Had to admit you could get fond of that Diana. Me and Noreen both, we reckoned she was getting like part of the family.

'You are quite an unpleasant young man,' went Caravella.

'That weren't nothing lady,' Noreen turned round and went. 'He hardly started yet. You want to hear him when he badmouth someone well and good.'

'And you — ' went Bernard to Noreen.

I was up there before he even thought it. No fucker gave the words to Noreen.

He caught my drift. 'Never mind for now,' he went. Then he cackled kind of nasty.

I sat down again. Catch him later.

'Well this is right handy innit,' I went. 'Here we fucking are. All together like. Three of you shafted your bro on my staircase. Most of Walthamstow knowing you did it. You knowing we knowing you did it. Only fuckers not knowing or not keen on knowing got to be Old Bill.'

Rupert pouring himself a drop of vino.

'So what's the story here?' I goes. 'Why you all in Wengen like the same time or what?'

'There is no cause at all for us to answer you,' went Caravella. 'You have told us nothing but calumnies.'

'Noreen?' I goes.

'Porkies,' she went. 'Calumnies is porkies.'

'Thank you Noreen. Now you start on the hearing out Caravella — '

'Miss Mannion,' went Rupert.

'Oh lah-di-dah,' goes Noreen, that kirsch gave her eyes on stalks.

'Now you hearing me out Caravella,' I carries on.

'Give you the straight goods here. Case you want it or not. That Diana hired me for finding out who wasted her hubbie. No problem. You three fuckers wasted her hubbie. Your bro. Bleedin' fuckin' obvious. So bleedin' obvious you been trying to give Diana and me the big word in our ear ever since you heard I was around. So now I gives you that question again before I kicks it out of you. The fuck you all here in Swiss?'

'Not that it is any of your business,' went Bernard, reasonable one. 'But obviously one comes to Wengen for New Year.'

'One does? Any special cause?'

'It is the DHO cocktail party tomorrow,' Caravella turned round and said. 'Before that it is the paper chase. Bernard of course has duties through his long tradition of public service. His duties to the parliamentary ski team combine happily with his obligations to the DHO. I am not sure why I bother to tell you this since you are clearly not in the membership of the DHO.'

'DHO?' I asked Noreen.

'Never heard of it Nicky.'

'DHO?' I went to the fuckers.

'Oh for God's sake,' went Rupert. 'Why are we talking to this oik? The DHO is the most important ski club in the country. There is only one other real club. Great Britain effectively invented skiing through the DHO.'

'Never heard that,' I went. 'But there I never got the time for a lot of skiing. Noreen though she's bleedin' ace innit? Noreen you a member of that UFO?'

'Never heard of it Nicky,' Noreen went again. 'Got to be one of them new agencies spring up every day, always say they been going years. Some cheap package out of Luton I expect.'

'The DHO', went Rupert loud, 'is the oldest ski club in the world! Here, here in Wengen we began downhill skiing — '

'I always reckoned it was that William Tell invented that skiing.'

'We will leave,' went Bernard. 'He is just provoking you Rupert, can't you see that? Probably trying to provoke some indiscretion. Or perhaps he is just like that by nature. Mr Burkett, I understand from my sister-in-law that is your name. You are in here over your head. If I were you I would leave Wengen tomorrow. My sister-in-law is too ill, sadly, to tell you herself — '

''Cause you pushed her under,' went Noreen. 'And I saw you!'

He went total shitfaced. Bit of a dodgy witness statement that one off Noreen, bit of a total Old Bill-type construction. Bit of a bad time in the bargain, maybe better she buttoned it right then. Put a bit of a gobsmack on Bernard though. Reckoned he might get a ticker job on the fucking spot, been a proper result. Instead they turned round and left. Shitfaced. Without any goodnights. Just when they got up the staff turned up again asking we wanted more of the refreshments.

We filled up on the wine, sent the rest off. Then we got a second thinking, called them back polite like. Yes, they reckoned they got another bottle of that kirsch downstairs.

Two hours later I reckoned Noreen was fit like a banshee. Long night ahead.

Problem was though when I got downstairs again I fell asleep across the bed before I even got my clobber off. Woke up the same way in the morning, Noreen somehow burrowed underneath.

15

'Jesus Noreen,' I went over my coffee, 'ain't it this brown bread in Wengen's something para? Take a loaf or two home for your mum and dad or what?'

'Right Nicky. Coffee a bit special too.'

Then they brought the cheese.

'Nah John,' I went to the waiter. 'Cheese for breakfast mate? I still got the gyp from last night believe it. No hard feelings geezer only you got any sugar puffs or what?'

'It is normal here in Switzerland,' he turns round and says. 'It is the smorga for us. Of course you may have the jam and marmalade and muesli and eggs and fruit instead if you are preferring. It is not compulsory the cheese.'

'Cheers mate,' I went. 'Glad to hear it.'

So we got the jam and marmalade and muesli and eggs and fruit. Muesli was crap, get better out of Food Giant. Rest was a result. We got about four pints of coffee in the bargain. Knew how to sort out a breakfast the Swiss.

Then John boy brought us the invites. First one came separate on a card. 'The DHO requests the pleasure of your company,' it went, 'at the Hotel Falken at 6.30 on New Year's Eve. Drinks.'

I passed it over Noreen.

'You reckon drinks got to mean them cocktails?' I went.

'Like as not Nicky. I got two more of them invitations here in one envelope. One's kind of a letter except nobody signed it. Wants you to take tea.'

'What else it says?'

' "Dear Mr Burkett, I wish to invite you to take tea on the terrace of the Hotel Edelweiss in Murren at four o'clock. You may learn something to your advantage." '

'Shit. And that other one? Want me to take anything?'

' "Dear Mr Burkett, I trust you and your lady will be able to join us for a private dinner party at Wengernalp at eight o'clock. If you yourself could stay behind afterwards I may explain matters. It is time to clear the air. Yours faithfully, Bernard Mannion." '

We let all that settle with the brown bread. 'Be a busy day,' I went.

'You going to them?' she went.

'When you find out for me where they all bleeding are Noreen.'

'I'm going skiing Nicky. And you got to have a lesson natural.'

217

'We fit it in. So you find the places and that, why I brought you here innit?'

'Nicky you notice how he put your lady on that letter? Notice how he never put your bird? You reckon you take notice of that? How some people maybe treat their women?'

'Ach Noreen, bird, lady, same difference. Now we best get cracking eh? Where you reckon I go for my skiing lesson?'

'I'll show you.' She started on giggling. 'Now you make sure you go to the toilet first Nicky. Get in all that ski gear you never get out again and make it worse you could get a bit nervous, make you want to wee like crazy. You take care of that or you want me to do your weeing for you as well?'

'You just look after your own weeing Noreen then you show me where that shop is, you catch my drift? We passed it yesterday innit?'

We went upstairs and got into the snow bits. She was wanting me putting on all her fucking underwear, not bleeding likely. Put on a tracksuit. She got two pairs of tights and vest and shirt and top then some ski suit I never knew she had then her woolly hat and shades and big mittens she was Michelin woman. I put my jacket on over the tracksuit, hard man. Ray-Bans course, you went skiing you got to be cool. Fortunate I nicked them one time before Noreen put a blank on the nicking. Put my gloves on I got from the army surplus. I was oiled.

Out the hotel and it was round the corner you booked the ski lesson, just where it was before. They reckoned they still got a few places left in the beginners'. Then they told me two shops where I could hire the gear. One across the street.

'Good morning sir.' Some way they reckoned I spoke English before I even opened my gob.

'All right mate? You help me out here? I got a ski lesson only I ain't got none of the gear. They reckon you fix me the works like no problem?'

'No problem at all sir. We will equip you from top to bottom. Fit you up like a bloody champion.'

I clocked him up then we both cackled. 'Right mate,' I goes, 'seems like you might be an all right geezer. Go to it Wilhelm, sort the bleeding business.'

He measured me up then he measured me round then he pushed and pulled and squeezed somehow giggling quiet all the while, asked me who I was and how I fancied their birds up there. Got me boots big enough and skis big enough and poles big enough, poles like you clocked on all the

219

photos. Shoved me in boots so tight I stopped feeling below the ankle, hoped they never dropped off. Clicked me into the skis wearing the boots. Clicked me out again, reckoned I wore the boots up the ski school only I got to carry the skis and poles. Fucking how was another question. Then I gave him so much dosh maybe I bought the whole shop some misunderstanding. Called for some little scam somewhere, emergency measures. Then he turned me toward the door, slapped me on the back and went, 'Go for it Lone Ranger!' Maybe they got some very old TV programmes out there.

'Thank you Tonto don't mind if I do,' I went.

Then I got out the door.

Then I fell arse over tit all over their snow. Jesus.

How the fuck you were supposed to stand up in their boots? Time I got up the school I was likely needing four pints of lager and a massage. I got standing took about twenty minutes. Then bent down for picking up the skis and poles, fell over again. Hooter went straight in the snow like a badger. No one took notice. Picked myself up. Took another two steps. Leaned on the pole, what they were for leaning on. Took another two. Stopped. Leaned.

Ski school behind the ice rink they reckoned. Fifty yards, time I got there I was so knackered all my muscles quivered. Sweat pouring so I never clocked the world through the Ray-Bans. Took them off. Spotted a group maybe a dozen birds and geezers. Beginners got to be.

One of them fit though. Taller than I was. Blonde. Muscles rippled. Serious.

'Hello,' she turned round and said. 'Have you come for my beginners' group? Are you Nicholas?'

'All right Heidi? Yeah only now I walked up here I got totalled already innit? You the boss then? Pleased to meet you and that, Jesus you're some fit bird you hear what I'm saying?' I was gabbling never even got my head straight. Wanted to lie down in their snow.

She started giggling in the bargain. 'In fact,' she went, 'my name is Trudi.'

'All right Trudi?'

'I can see you and I we are going to get along just fine. You will give me a bit of a good laugh I am thinking. Did you get dressed up like so just now or are you coming from England like that?' Then she started chortling again, never stopped all morning every time she clocked me. Bit of all right was that Trudi.

We started on some exercises.

Four English geezers there, pity two of them Scousers. Couple of Krauts got Frankfurt on their jackets, never made them hard. Four Swiss, one a geezer the rest old biddies. Fit old biddies. Ages added up to four hundred and fifty. Then there was me.

You swung your arms round. Even in her ski suit you could clock all Trudi's bits move. Gave me a cold sweat. So we swung arms a bit more then we swung our legs. Not easy, all the Brits fell over. Then Trudi reckoned we put our skis on.

Fucking doss on the telly putting your skis on. Not so easy in real life.

Trudi came over knelt by my knee on account of my foot never got clicked in that ski.

'Why is your leg shaking like that?' she goes. 'Are you suffering from hypothermia?'

'Call it that Trudi. Comes over me whenever birds get kneeling round my pins. Kind of fever.'

'Ah-ha you are so funny. Now that is your two skis.' She raised her voicebox for the rest. 'Now I want you all to follow me by walking over to that post.'

Few yards off no problem that post. I set off took a step forward. Then another and another and another. Fucking strange how I took all those steps forward only finished up ten yards further back.

Most of the party made it sort of halfway only a few got major aggravation. Trudi came skiing down cackling fit to bust, got hold of my mitt and hauled me over her snow up by that post. I hung on to it save disappearing downtown.

'All right now. Sometimes it is more easy to walk up a hill by going sideways. Do this for me please. Let me see you all walk up to me now moving your legs sideways up the hill.'

Jesus H. Christ. And his mum. This skiing business got more to it than you reckoned. I took one step sideways up that mountain. Needed a fucking crane for it. Got the right ski there then lifted the other one. Shit. Whoops. Whoa . . . I was going round in a fucking circle now, spinning down that mountain headed for fucking sea level.

Best entertainment that Trudi got in years, ought to charge admission. 'Oh Nicholas,' she cried when she caught up, 'you are a case isn't it? My baby is better at skiing than you are my dear . . . '

'So how old's your baby then lady? Going on eighteen or what?'

'Two months only Nicholas.'

Two months? Kind of a fit bird here?

'Jesus Trudi. You interrupt the ski lesson for

having that baby or you just whip it out quick on some slalom am I right?'

'Nicholas you are not having the faintest clue what a slalom is. Is that so? You are taking the piss?' She made with the sweet smile. Knew she had the fucking whip over me any time she wanted. Ratbag.

'All right everyone! Now that we all can stand up straight I am going to take you up to the top of this nursery slope. You give the kind man at the bottom one franc to use his mini-ski-lift. Then you are all going to ski down again, nice and gently I am thinking.'

Shit. Fucking nursery slope looked about a thousand feet high.

'When you reach to the bottom of the slope you must stop at the ice rink. I will show you how to stop. It is like this with your skis. Please try to learn this or you will be practising your first ski jump right over the ice rink and into your hotel bedrooms I am thinking. Please pay attention Nicholas.'

'Who me?'

'When we get to the top of the slope you will remember two things please. When you lean to the right you turn to the left. Like so.' She gave it the demo and we tried it out going to the geezer with his ski-lift. 'And when you lean to the left you will turn to the right. Like so. Are you all understanding that?

Thank you. The other point I am telling you again after that is how you stop with the skis. Like so. Good. We are all ready?'

Nobody daring giving her the no-no. We practised that stopping like no one's business. Then we waddled over the geezer, gave him his dosh. He showed us where you stood for the lift. You got to grab it in one hand when it came past only hang on your poles in the other. Near as wrenched my shoulder out its socket, no problem.

Lift took us fifty yards up the slope. We all stood there together. All ready. Clocking around.

Course the fucking Krauts got to be going first. Probably score a fucking goal the same time. No arguing.

They went off nicely nicely, doing fine. Then one fucker crashed into the mountain halfway down, definite result so we all howled. Old Swiss biddies jumped up and down cackling, never liked the Krauts. So Fritz got up serious vex, blood on his boat race. We howled some more.

Swiss biddies went next, put on a straight viz, make sure no death on the slopes. They all got down the bottom nice and steady.

Brits made a fair shot like you expect. Scousers fell over straight off. Never knew they were upset or not on account of they kept talking Scouse language, no one understand it. Carried on made the bottom eventual.

Last came Walthamstow.

I set off crouching like they did on the news. Sure and steady I went off down that hill.

I leaned to the right, turned to the left no worries. Cracked it.

I leaned to the left . . . only I still turned to the left. Fucking plan never worked, they sold me a pup. Kept leaning left, still turned left, no, wham! Straight in the bleeding mountain. Never mind eh. Up again, never let them spot your pain, give it some wellie here. Down that fucking nursery mountain.

No leaning left or right now, only get on down straight up. Straight for Trudi stood there in front that ice rink. Gently gently. One line straight in that snow.

How she said it was you stopped?

I turned in my toes how she did it. Turned them in so they fucking touched. How you did it. So what was the fucking problem here?

I was going quicker not stopping. One ski stuck over the other. Still quicker. Just then up came a little rise. Fucking skis total locked together now. Still pointed in though ought to be stopping. Never did.

Leaned right over stuck my hands out

trying to stick the poles in for stopping. We went quicker and quicker. We hit that rise. Skis went straight down in that snow.

They made their skis special so you ejected when they stuck. I ejected. Fact was instead of ejecting up I ejected horizontal. Like a bullet. Over that rise I was a fucking human torpedo. I went through their air like I was turbo-charged.

Tried to yell only nothing came out. Trudi stood there looking up still chortling. Too late for her moving, too late she clocked what was happening here.

Like a flying pig I hit her straight in her belly with my hooter. Forty miles an hour, she went down like she got nuked.

I was lying on top of her. My Judge Dread on her chest. And she was never moving.

I killed her?

I moved my gob over her left tit. Dead she never minded made no difference. Felt pretty fucking ace even through her ski suit.

Then underneath me she started up shaking slightly. Then more of it. Then started out cackling out loud. Then she was hooting and hollering like it went out of style. Seemed like the best bit of laugh they got in Switzerland for years.

'My dear dear Nicholas!' she went. 'Only my baby is allowed to put his mouth there!

Oh my! You are such a champion skier you have invented a new style of skiing, it is the ski jump without skis! You will be the champion of the world!'

You got to say she was taking liberties here, me being a serious geezer due some respect. Still I had to howl along with her and we lay on our backs in their snow till tears ran out of our beadies made a health hazard, turned to ice all over their ski runs.

Concluded the lesson.

★   ★   ★

I headed back the shop for dumping the gear. I lifted up each leg like it was full of my mum's rice pudding. Faced up all the geezers on the High Street, make sure no one getting their rocks off mocking me.

Then who the fuck was it coming out the souvenir shop? Only Tweedledum and fucking Tweedledummer.

Got over their injuries then. Well, got over them so they were walking. Tweedledum got a flat nose, Tweedledummer got tape over where his ears went. They both looked like fortune turned them bitter against the world. They were never smiling.

Behind them Mickey Cousins. Camel hair coat ready for action, only camel hair coat in

Wengen. Looked like a camel.

Fortunate I got disguised in my ski gear, hardly knew who I was myself. Heart went pumping. The fuck they doing here?

They went down the road away from the station, maybe heading some hotel not as nobby as Silberhorn, not got their own suite. I plodded up the ski shop. All my gear undamaged so I got enough dosh back for a deposit on a round the world trip. Coming out again without the clobber on felt like taking off. I limped back the hotel and lay down.

Mickey fucking Cousins and his boys.

I went asleep. Still only twelve o'clock only I skipped dinner. Had a nice snooze, woke up again two o'clock ready for nothing.

16

'Noreen!' I cried out. 'Leave it out they got to be having a bleedin' laugh!'

'What's your problem now Nicky?'

'I ain't going up there!'

Noreen came back off her morning skiing bouncy bouncy so you reckoned she just took a tab. Except her skin shone and her eyes shone and probably her little tits shone if you only got the energy for looking. She got a sarnie for dinner some place up the mountain she reckoned. I got my sleep for dinner. She got in the shower and I went back to sleep for pudding. Then we got slowly out the hotel then on their train down the valley for Lauterbrunnen. You got to go down the valley for getting up the other side where we got the invite for taking tea. Reckon they never thought they might build a bridge.

'I ain't never going up there!' I told her. 'You seen that fuckin' machine Noreen?'

'That little train Nicky? So you got a problem with a little train now?'

'Little train? Little train about right innit? Little tin box and only goes straight up that mountain? You seen it? Not like that little train up Wengen Noreen, winding winding nice and gentle. Only going straight up in a straight line this one? Nothing for stopping it falling straight back down again? No way Noreen they got to be makin' joke here you hear what I'm saying?'

We got out the main station down Lauterbrunnen then walked over their road for the shed they reckoned was the station up Murren.

'Nicky you a big man.'

'Now be fair Noreen . . . '

'You got a rep in some places?'

'Nah! I ain't going up there!'

'You trust me to tell everyone you ever met round Walthamstow you were too scared to get in a train?'

'Some train up the sky! Suicide mission!'

'Nicky give me your hand.'

'Oh Gawd.'

'Otherwise you got to climb up through the woods to get there. They got bears and wolves in them forests Nicky. And man-eating deer so I heard.'

'Noreen . . . '

She bought tickets. We went in the shed for going up the death ride. Train came right down in the shed. We got in sat down. Fuck. I started getting air sick. I shut my mince pies. That train started off. I kept them shut.

'Noreen . . . ' I went.

'Shhh Nicky dear,' went Noreen holding my little glove in hers and patting it up. 'Don't you worry.' She went on patting it. I set my brain to thinking on a pint of lager down the boozer on Hoe Street. I never thought about that sky underneath us.

Then the fucker stopped.

'We stuck?' I went. 'We in mid-air? We got to jump?'

'Nicky it's a train. We not in mid-air. We there. You can get out now.'

I opened my beadies. Never ought to just there. I clocked all the way down the mountain we just came up. 'Yaah!' I went. Then we got out. We were still beating.

'No problem Noreen,' I went. 'No problem at all, little ride up.'

They got another train waiting for us only this one was normal on the flat.

'Yeah Noreen,' I went. 'Easy peasy innit. Bonza. Another train just what the fucking doctor ordered eh?'

Few Swiss schoolkids clocking me strange. Fuck 'em.

Five minutes later on that flat train through the forests we were in Murren.

Like a picture postcard.

Murren on top of their cliffs looking out the mountains. Blue sky shone. Rows of mountains snow all over them behind. Nearest one bleeding beautiful, tumbling down snow all over. Far side of it two more, different style more like straight up. Noreen reckoned one was that Eiger, she got near it in the morning. Round Murren they got green fields so their postcards reckoned. Now all under snow. More snow than they got in Wengen. Across the valley Wengen sat there lower down, still see it not dark yet. We went strolling round Murren like you do.

Two streets they got in Murren, met both ends. We walked all down one. They got ski-lifts. Case you were total loose in the brain area they even got a cable car. We clocked it. It came out the sky it went up in the sky. You could hear Noreen's little mind tick over, winding her geezer up. She shot me one under the lashes. Edges of her gob started quivering. Then she turned away a moment, sudden attack of coughing. Never even dared suggesting it, sensible bird.

Past their sports centre and shops. Quiet like a judge. Still they never cleared the pavements. We got up the end then came back down the other street spotting all their hotels. And there it was. Got a terrace. Sit out in the freezer, Hotel Edelweiss.

So we sat there by a table on their terrace. Ten to four.

'I just go in the toilet a minute get cleaned up,' goes Noreen. 'You order me a coffee Nicky.'

'Who me? In that German? And you just got cleaned up in our suite.'

'In German Nicky. And maybe a little cake? Slice of one of them fruit tarts?'

'Be thankful you get the coffee.'

She went off in the hotel. Smart move, fucking freezing outdoors. No one else outside now the sun went in behind the mountains. No one not even a waiter.

Except Caravella. She came off the street.

'Walk this way,' she went.

She got a shooter in her paw.

Some little woman's gun I never recognized. Trouble with woman's guns though they were never like woman, they never shot you gentle like when you made promise-I-never-do-it-again-please-forgive-me-give-me-one-more-chance-no-problem. Shot with a woman's gun and you got just as dead as a geezer's gun. Wrong name for it. Just on account of it was little never made it like a woman.

She brought it on the plane they wanted to check their X-rays. Or she came in a motor. Never made a fucking lot of difference now anyhow, it was a shooter and she got it on me and everyone else in Murren was in keeping warm.

'Fuck off,' I went brave.

She shot past me quiet into the valley. Shooter was quiet. I was quiet.

When you got a geezer with a shooter he always wanted for telling you the story before he shot you. So I heard. Another problem her being a woman it looked like. Wanted to do the business straight off no bigmouthing.

I went down on the street where she pointed. I tried the nicely nicely.

'You looking good today Caravella,' I turned round and said. 'Only you looking a bit mean girl. You got woman's problems? You got one of them migraines? You want to talk about it?'

'Move,' she went.

We moved down the road a few steps.

'Jump down there,' she went.

By the hotel they got a three-foot drop inside an alley. I dropped. She dropped. She never slipped and I never kicked off.

It was cold and it was wet. Wet all round my knees. Bottled all over my body. This was it. End of story.

I turned round trying reasoning with her more. 'Caravella,' I started off saying.

Then I clocked something behind her.

Jesus.

'Caravella,' I went again. 'You want to tell me what this business all about or what?'

She shot past me again. Gave me the nod for keeping going.

We went twenty yards through a bit of garden then headed for a little field and woods. I went slow, slow as you could. Down in the snow. Looking for time. It was never far enough. We crossed that field her pointing from behind. Walked on. Up to the trees then went in. Took under a minute. I knew what came after the trees and I never liked it.

Nothing. No fucking thing.

'Walk,' she went again.

'Caravella you not serious.'

'Walk.'

She wanted me over the edge. Shoot me she never minded only she preferred never leaving a mark. Wanted me flying.

I reckoned I got to make my moves and it got to be pretty fucking quick. Nothing to lose now. Get shot or get bounced on a rock two thousand feet down. Make a choice. We were getting through the trees.

It was there.

Then she made her mistake. She reckoned she was a geezer. She got to yack about it.

'You think you know it all,' she went. 'People like you. You think it is easy for us. You think we don't know struggle and fear and loneliness. We had it hard I can tell you

236

when we were young — '

'Give a shit,' I went.

'You think you know what Oliver was like. You think bloody Diana is a bloody saint. Well, let me tell you there are two sides to every story.'

'You want to tell me about it?'

'No! You are an interfering busybody and there is only one way to deal with you. The others may have wanted to negotiate with you but — '

I dived.

She heard him behind close. She clocked him. Then she backed and shot. I was scrabbling, down the floor crawling scratching hustling off. I never looked back what was happening there.

Then a whine came out her like I never could miss and never could forget. Whine disappearing.

I turned round. She was gone.

And there was a huge great fucking pause.

And we looked up each other me and him.

'Fuckin' hell TT,' I went, 'where the fuck you been you useless bleedin' fucker? She near as croaked me you fuckin' heap of fuckin' shit and where were you eh?'

I shook.

'My God,' he went. Pause. 'She's gone.'

'Yeah she fuckin' gone TT no doubting about that mate.'

'My God.' Pause. 'Do you know how far it is Nicky down there?'

'Never make no fuckin' difference TT. Few thousand feet what the fuck? She gone.'

'Oh my God.'

'You fuckin' turned round and said that. Now we best advised fucking the hell out of here. We get up that terrace and you get a fuckin' coffee and then you turn round and tell me just what the fuck you doing here at all. I was just managing nicely till you turn up, only just talking her down no problem. Then you get her all vex like that then she drop off.' Best I get a few facts clear from the start off.

'Nicky we've got obligations. I'm a police officer — '

'Not here you're bleeding not TT. So you get the fuck out of this alley and hope it fuckin' snows or whatever, cover up your footmarks eh?'

'Oh my God.'

I got him up the Edelweiss. He shook now.

'Where you been Nicky I'm bleeding freezing!' goes Noreen sat on the terrace. 'Nicky ... bleeding hell, that you TT or what?'

'One and the same,' I goes.

'What you doing here TT?'

'I, er, I came . . . I thought I'd best come because I might be able to give you an assist Nicky — '

'You mean seeing as how you landed us in this heap of shit maybe you owed us one get us out again or what?'

'Well Nicky . . . '

'Let's get indoors,' went Noreen, 'out of this snow. Jesus TT you look white as a sheet man, you seen a ghost or what?'

We got indoors. TT kind of shaky sat there for a coffee. I got a very urgent bowel problem up their toilets. Not connected to events course, got to be that cheese fighting back.

TT eh. Never thought I'd be happy clocking a fucking pig.

* * *

TT was staying down in the valley up Lauterbrunnen. Not on expenses so he was down the fucking campsite. Pretty fucking amusing that, we reckoned he could come up our suite for sitting in some warm air he wanted. Not long though. Once a pig always a pig.

He was all shook up. Soft as shit these days Old Bill, never even handle a trauma.

He was worrying on how he got to liaise up the local station. He was worrying about when they found the body. Fuck the body. He was worrying about his missis and kids when he spent a life sentence in a Swiss nick. He was never worrying what he was doing New Year's Eve more to the point. Maybe find him some willing Swiss biddy do a bit of abseiling practice. We got to distract him.

'TT,' went Noreen, 'we heard everyone gets together up Wengen in their square about eleven-thirty on New Year's Eve, you want to be up there? Get some of them celebrations? Be cool innit TT? Few drinks, bit of raving and that? You up for it?'

'God I don't know. Maybe. Thank you very much.'

We went off for the station up Murren. Then all of a sudden we were down Lauterbrunnen. I came down that train thinking on TT and I never gave that mountain one moment's consideration, not one minute. We were down the bottom. Shit.

TT ready to walk down his Camping Jungfrau. Only he was never ready for leaving us he was so fucking worrying. We had to go getting another coffee across the street before he was bold enough and we could get back up Wengen.

And who the fuck was in the café where we got the coffee?

Boxers.

Boxers I last clocked down that hospital ward. Before that getting shot round the Tamil gaff. That Nellie got the scars on his bonce where Jimmy put the vase in. Next one still like half unconscious, staring in space.

Tell the third by how he was standing. Probably never ever sit down again, serious bum problem.

Bright geezers all of them. Likely not too sure what they came up Switzerland for only knowing they got to be fierce. Clocked me now. Gave me the stare.

I sat on their table. TT and Noreen sat down in the bargain never knowing. Noreen ordered coffees.

'Evening fellers,' I went.

Never answer. Three geezers quiet.

'Fuck off,' goes Nellie eventual. Got to be the thinker.

'Come up Swiss for the rucking fellers? Break a few hooters keep your hand in?'

'Fuck.'

'Or try the muesli and a bit of banking?'

They got up together. Very slowly. Did some looming.

'Introduce my old mate DS Holdsworth, Chingford nick. Close links with Interpol.

Show the fuckers your badge TT.'

He fucking did too.

They sat down together.

'Geezers never mean me no good TT,' I turned round and said. 'Contract off our friends what you know about I reckon. Am I right geezers? Noreen you got your camera with you, take a few snaps of us together here?'

They were gone. Slowly.

Shit. We got large problems up Wengen. It was cooking.

17

We got in our suite again, just about time for a shower and a spot of nookie before we got up that cocktail party. What you did after a day in the mountains so I heard, had a little lie down. We got up again and asked the way up the Hotel Falken. William Tell and Heidi both off duty again behind the desk. Got a geezer told you the exact distance up the Hotel Falken and what they got for tea. He pointed it and we found it.

Noreen looking like a million francs when she walked in that door. In the hotel, directed up their function room, through the door into a big bubbling mess of white charlies. Noreen never gave a shit. Only black bird or geezer in the place and she never gave a monkey's when they stopped and gawped like their champagne curdled. Then they started in on the big friend-up, show how they were never prejudiced. Fucking diamond that Noreen.

Course it helped her being a fit bird.

Geezer came bumbling up to us, little bumbly geezer, check our invite and give us the welcome. He got a scarf round his neck maybe caught a rash. 'How nice to have you here with us tonight,' he goes. 'I am Francis McAlpine, secretary of the DHO. How nice that you could come. Who do you know here? Do you know the Levines over there or maybe the Jacobsons? I believe they hail from your part of the world.'

He never knew we spoke English leave alone what part of the world we did our hailing in. Put us down for Hampstead types probably. 'You a secretary in the bargain?' I goes. 'Noreen here she's one of them innit? Know that geezer over there now you come to mention it. Geezer with the long conk.'

'Who was that?'

'My mate Rupert.' I raised my tones. 'Rupert!'

Eight geezers swung round and clocked me.

'Oh you must never call out that word in here,' goes the sec. 'They're all called Rupert here you see, it's part of the territory. Perhaps you could go over and tap him on the arm if you would like his attention.'

'Perhaps I could. Only first mate you point me out where a geezer gets a Pernod round here? Booze on the freeman's you hear what I'm saying?'

'Er, the bar is just round the corner, is that what you were asking? Now if you would excuse me I do believe the Battles have just come in and I must go over to make them welcome. You probably know of their unfortunate mishap in the City . . . '

'Fair enough John no problem. Catch you later.' We set off for the drink through the crowd.

And they got a full crowd in. All the geezers got scarves round their necks you couldn't help but notice, maybe an epidemic that rash. All the birds though they got long necks like they spent the day trying to see over some wall. Never natural it was. And when they laughed it was like someone squeezed on their neck in the bargain.

Our Rupert never wanted to know when he clocked us. Bernard though he was there with him and he was Mr Olive Oil. He came over smooth.

'Ah. I am so glad to see that you were able to come,' he goes.

'No problem mate, fit you in. Fancy a pint?'

'Actually my glass is full at the moment. I don't suppose you have seen my sister Caravella on your travels today?'

'Caravella? Now you come to mention it I do believe I did. Only we popped up Murren ain't that right Noreen, popped up there for a train ride out and I reckon I did clock that

Caravella somewhere only I got the impression she was going off somewhere very hasty. Never turned round and said so much as a by your leave. Tell you what Bernard mate, I reckon you got saddled with that Rupert and Caravella, you hear what I'm saying? You being a geezer of class and that, you want to do yourself a favour mate, get rid of them innit? Not in your league am I right? Now for a start-off that Rupert — '

'Thank you Mr Burkett I think I can make my own decisions about my family without your assistance. I will see you later at Wengernalp when we can have a chat after dinner, just you and me alone, and you can give me the invaluable benefit of your views. Now if you will excuse me . . . '

'No problem mate. Consider yourself excused.'

He went off.

'Nicky,' went Noreen.

'Yes my darling?'

'None of that darling darling Nicky. You saw that Caravella in Murren?'

'Well Noreen . . . '

'And none of them wells.'

'Well Noreen she may just have got one moment in my line of vision, you hear what I'm saying?'

'And you never happened to mention it?'

'That right? That the case I never mentioned it? Well now you turn round and say so I suppose that is true words, maybe I never. Make sure I do better next time innit?'

'Nicky you been out committing them crimes again?'

'Never Noreen you know that. Not even one. Not even one little one.'

''Cause they count in Switzerland just the same as they count in Walthamstow, you understand that? Crime is a crime.'

'Crime is a crime Noreen quite right girl. No messing.'

'Got to believe you Nicky,' went Noreen snuggling up. 'Knew you wouldn't tell me a straight porkie. All sorts of ways round the truth maybe but never a straight porkie, correct?'

'Correct Noreen.' Made me a bit uncomfortable though.

One thing you got to notice on the birds and geezers up their DHO. Not one of them looked a bit like a fucking skier. None of them fit. Nor brown. Nor wearing goggles and squinting. Nor talking sexy and shafting everything on two legs.

They got a geezer in a dog collar there. Supping a pint by the bar looking cheery. He gave me the church grin.

'Bless you father,' I goes.

'I beg your pardon?'

'No problem John. Carry on.'

'Allow me to introduce myself. I am the resident Church of England minister in Wengen.'

'We all got our cross to bear mate. Fancy another one of them?'

'Well, thank you . . . I don't mind if I do. You are one of the, er, newer DHO members I take it?'

'Just visiting. Me and Noreen here. Take in a spot of skiing, bit of the old boozing, know how it is.'

'Of course. Now if you will excuse me . . . ' He got sudden called away before he even got his freeman's.

Then Rameez walked in.

Jesus H. Christ and his missis.

Rameez geared up like a fucking footballer appearing in court on a bribe charge. He got a silver suit on and a waistcoat spingle spangly like a shower of smarties. He got rings on every finger. He got hair shiny like he stood under a waterfall. He got brothel creeper shoes on and underpants so tight his parts stood out like they just got lit up.

A little sigh went round that room.

'Jesus H. Christ and his missis,' I goes. 'Rameez.'

'Yo Nicky! You the man!'

'Rameez . . . the fuck you doing here Rameez?'

'Came to give you my assist Nicky course. Heard you might be needing myself.'

'And get your mitts on them expenses.'

'And take part in one earned share of those expenses suffered in the line of duty Nicky.'

'You got an invite to this party? This some special do, invite only.'

'Course I got an invite Nicky you reckon I come in here uninvited? Bad manners innit? Borrowed one invite off some geezer I happened to come across down by that station who never seemed to have no special need of it so I made one little suggestion to him on the subject.'

'Like he better fuck off before you gouged him?'

'Nicky let us not get into all the nitty gritty details man eh? I heard you might be needing an assist. I here. Right?'

'You heard off TT?'

'Rameez,' goes Noreen interrupting coming from the bar where she bought our drinks. She got Rameez a Pernod when she clocked him.

'Good evening Noreen.' Her always making Rameez nervous.

'You come out here committing crimes?'

'Noreen the sun shines, the wind blows, a

businessman does business innit?'

'Very philosophical Rameez. Only don't you be taking Nicky on that business.' Then she left us one minute. Round about two dozen geezers wanting to be buying her drinks and dribbling on her, she got to take time out.

'Nicky you got to see this new blade I bought up Zurich,' Rameez goes pulling me in a corner. 'Four hundred fucking years old man, stars and moons down the sheath like the holy flag of Pakistan, two feet long and it cut your hooter off clean as a fucking whistle Nicky I'm telling you.'

Rameez always got this thing about slicing. Other geezers got an enemy they stab him. Rameez always wanting to chop a few bits off.

'You got it here?'

'Yeah man.'

'Where?'

'Down my fucking leg course where you think?'

'I lend it?'

'Nicky it being worth about one thousand of their little francs.'

'Give you Noreen as security.'

'Ha ha Nicky! Even you telling the truth, which you ain't, you reckon I last five minutes with Noreen? She a very disapproving woman Nicky. Not got a lot of respect for a geezer of status, know what I mean?'

'Know what you mean Rameez. Borrow me the blade?'

'Course Nicky you got the need. You want it now?'

'I got to get up Wengernalp. You see after Noreen Rameez. I not back by midnight you come running, got it?'

'You want I send Aftab and Afzal up?'

'What?'

'Yeah they here Nicky. No problem man.'

'Jesus . . . Nah. Keep them ready, right? TT be here later.' I took the blade off him and got ready for fucking off out. Bernard and Rupert already gone.

Noreen came back. 'You going up that place Nicky?' she goes.

'Best I go, see what they wanting. You coming too like you were invited?'

'You take Paulette with you.'

'Paulette . . . '

'Yeah Paulette. She waiting outside.'

'Paulette James?'

'How many Paulettes you know Nicky? Yeah course Paulette James. Got her out here for a bit of support. Support for me another girl innit? Support for you Nicky more to the point 'cause I got her out here to watch your back you know. Be your minder in certain situations. Being as she's a girl she can go with you like social things, still give you protection where she's a big girl and you being only midgy. And where I wouldn't be no use.'

'Jesus Noreen.'

'And where I know you wouldn't ever try it on with Paulette either.'

'Noreen I just turned down Aftab and Afzal off Rameez for tonight.'

'She waiting outside in the cold watching your back already. You be taking Paulette Nicky.'

I took Paulette. She got muscles in places you never thought of. I put on all the clobber and got outside in the freezer. Paulette standing there already on sentry duty. Never felt the cold it seemed like.

'Yo Paulette.'

'Yo Nicky.'

'You the minder I heard.'

'Wipe your bum Nicky, stop you falling down some snow drift, see you right.' One problem with Paulette was she never took me serious. Since we were eight years old and she gave me a start of fifty metres over a hundred, still beat me by thirty, she never took me serious. Always left her cackling. Me I blamed the cigarettes.

I never even asked her for a touch of the other, Paulette. Hard when they never take you serious. Never do it cackling fit to bust.

We got the train up Wengernalp.

They invited us for eight o'clock. We got there half past. Wengernalp was some restaurant halfway up the mountain middle of nowhere. Trains still running on New Year's Eve. Nice little train again, none of that vertical shit, wound up nice and gentle through the trees. Started snowing.

'Nicky,' goes Paulette, breathing in mountains, altitude training.

'Yes Paulette.'

'These trains are stopping soon. You gave any thought to how it is we getting down again?'

'Nah Paulette. Never gave it any thought.'

'What I reckoned Nicky.'

We had a bit of a pause there. Not a lot to add. Get down somehow no doubting.

We stopped outside their restaurant up Wengernalp and got off that train. Only ones getting off. We went over the building, kind of a barn. Train started off again up the mountain where they got some bigger place. We went in the door.

Guess what they got for dinner. Fucking cheese sauce.

'Do you like fondue?' they all went.

'Champion mate,' I goes. 'Nothing better.'

There was a dozen of them. Private party.

Bernard and his mistress, bird they missed when they gave out the chins. Name of Tanya. Rupert and his bit of stuff, only her they gave too many chins maybe got Tanya's mixed up in them. Eight others there, all couples all Brits. All talked like they got strangled earlier in the evening.

'This is your lady?' goes Bernard.

'Yeah this my bird. Bit of all right innit?' Paulette mash me up later. 'She never could turn down an invite.' Bernard clocked Noreen all night last night then again down the DHO. On the other hand none of them ever could tell the difference, one black bird looked just the same as another. Paulette twice the size maybe, apart from that. Or maybe he reckoned I got a lot of women.

We dipped in that fondue. I was still never keen on dipping with the fuckers getting their spit all in my sauce. I got some salad and that brown bread. Bit of vino. Looked round for some of that kirsch, none in sight. They were all yacking on about their skiing and would you believe it the schools they sent their fucking kids to. Imagine my mum going on about McEntee or Monoux or where the fuck. Then they got their fruit flans out, cherries and that. And the cheese. More cheese.

'Tell me,' went some bird name of Fiona,

deciding on friending us up. 'I believe you both come from Walthamstow. Do tell me what life is like in Walthamstow.'

''Scuse us lady?'

'Tell me what it is like to live there in the present day. Is it still one great community that you are part of? Pie and mash shops, street parties, that kind of thing? I do think we have lost something in leaving that kind of atmosphere behind. Is there a lot of crime there or do you all police the community yourselves, tight knit?'

Paulette clocked me. 'There a lot of crime Nicky?' she goes.

'Not enough mate. Not half bleeding enough.' They all listened up now. 'Them opportunities they aren't half the same as they were when we was young. Fucking Neighbourhood Watch, security crawling all over the precinct, trackers on all the fit motors, you never get the chance for doing a decent bit of work these days, know what I mean?'

'Yes of course,' went the bird. 'I know exactly what you mean. Deprivation. Lack of stimulation.'

'On the spot mate,' I goes. 'Deprivation. Too much of it about these days. And that stimulation. Everywhere.'

They were asking Bernard about that

Parliament, who was getting the freebies and considerations and backhanders. He reckoned you played your cards right you got on some committee, took some trip, few popsies waiting on the road, then you come home and they put your name up on some company for ten big ones every year. All you did after that was sign a few letters and smooth the path so the weapons got out there. Not too hard.

We sat there keeping our lugs open and our gobs shut. They brought out the coffee and brandy and then that kirsch again after all. I emptied my water glass back in the jug and filled up on it. Soothed down nice and warm.

'Well,' one of the geezers turned round and said eventual, 'perhaps we should be getting back in time for the festivities. That was delightful Bernard. A very pleasant occasion to celebrate your good fortune. Skiing back down again now will be the perfect way to end the evening.'

How they were getting back. Skiing, course.

Then they put all their suits on and torches on their Judge Dreads like miners. We got ready for moving in the bargain.

'Perhaps you and your lady would like to stay behind,' went Bernard. 'We could have a chat as I mentioned and you might learn something to your advantage.'

We sat down again. The geezers already went who served up the meal. Do the washing up in the morning. They never fussed about locking the shop, no one coming up the mountain in the middle of the night. Now everyone else went off. Bernard and Rupert sent their totties off. Only Paulette and me were left with them. We made our moves on the kirsch.

Then they got the hunting rifles out.

Kind of place for hunting rifles. Pictures on the walls of hunters carrying some dead animal down the mountain round their shoulders. No snow, summer activity. Still you got to keep the rifles somewhere in winter.

'They work them things?' I went. 'Or you just sniff powder through them?'

'We told you,' goes Bernard, 'that you would learn something to your advantage here. That will be true. However, you may also learn something to your disadvantage.'

'Just shoot the little bastard Bernard,' goes Rupert. 'Don't tell him anything. Shoot him and we'll dispose of him.'

'Paulette you got your javelin?' I went.

'I'm a runner Nicky not a bleeding thrower. Who the fuck do these jerks think they are anyway? Nobodies. I never even heard of them. They want to mess with me?'

'How about that triple jump, you do one of them on that Rupert?'

Rupert fired his rifle. It worked. Left a hole in the wall. Very silly move.

'Rupert!' went Bernard, understood it all. 'Not yet! Not here!'

But we lipped it for a bit. They simmered down.

So there we were. Bernard and Rupert on one side of the table, Rupert out of control and already left some evidence. Me and Paulette on the other side. They got rifles. We were stupid. I was stupid, got Paulette into this. Paulette was vex. I was shitless. Any way out of this fucker? It was never looking shiny.

'You see,' Bernard carried on calmer, 'you have been a nuisance to us. Our brother Oliver came to you to try to do some spying on us.'

'Good reason it turned out.'

'Yes, you could say that.'

'I just did mate.'

'It is true that we had a plan for him and so he had a reason to investigate, seen in his terms. Unfortunately when we became aware of his inquiries we were obliged to bring the plan forward. And escalate it.'

'Whack him.'

'It was very unfortunate that Oliver would not see reason.'

'Bastard,' goes Rupert. 'He wanted it all for himself. Stupid selfish unfair unreasoning bastard.'

'You see,' carries on Bernard. 'It was the usual inheritance problems. You know how it is.'

'Can't say as I do mate. Inheritance problems is one problem we never got round Walthamstow. Few other problems only not them inheritance problems.'

'Oliver being the eldest son you understand. And being married to Diana.'

'Bitch,' goes Rupert.

'Diana who you tried to waste in the bargain,' I goes.

'He intended that all the family fortune should go to her and their children.'

'Diana got kids?'

'Six of them. Whereas anyone could see that it should never all have gone to the eldest son in this day and age. All we wanted was to negotiate. We wanted nothing unreasonable, perhaps five mills each and leave him with the lion's share of the estate. But he would just not be reasonable.'

'Paulette,' I goes.

'Yes Nicky?'

'When I say run, you fuck off, right?' They

both heard. No point whispering.

I threw Rameez's blade. First time in my fucking life I threw a blade and then I got to get it out the sheath, fucking great thing took about a fortnight. I reckoned Bernard was more dangerous, Rupert more jumpy.

'Run!'

Blade stuck in Rupert's arm. Bernard was between us and the door. Just one moment he turned to clock Rupert. Paulette kicked him in the bollocks, he went down and she was gone.

I was after but Bernard was up again before the door. I got hold close and hung on. Rifle up tight in his hand, never use it. I swung him round between me and Rupert, stop Rupert firing when he pulled the blade out. Bernard grabbed hold to turn me back. I butted him hard. First time it ever worked for me, normally I only whacked myself on the hooter. He fell away and I was out of there.

Paulette was gone, right. They never catch her.

I got only my shirt and jeans and trainers on. There was the train track maybe I should take for running on. There was a wide path by it only it was all iced over. Then I got it. Toboggan run.

Beside the restaurant was a sledge. I ran and grabbed it, hauled it on the path. I heard them come out behind me. Then I was down flat on it and sliding. Just one moment I was a dead target for them. Fucking cracking noise rifles make. Two of them.

Missed. One hit the sledge. I was gone.

Only the fucking sledge was all over the fucking toboggan run. Fifteen years since I was on a sledge and now I was shitless, speeding down there all over the fucking shop. Bump one side, bump the other. I hit the side full on one moment. Stopped and looked round. They were coming down on skis after me and they were carrying their rifles.

It was snowing and it was dark only it was light. I went off again. Now I reckoned I was learning this fucking sledge. Foot down, swerve. Other foot, swerve. Hoped it went better than skiing.

Another crack off a rifle. Not a fucking chance here. They got to stop for aiming and then they lost time. When they never stopped though they were gaining. Getting closer.

We were gone maybe half a mile from the eater now. Then shit. Everything turning to the right, the whole track and railway on a big right curve. Everything except me. The sledge hit the bank hard. I went straight on over. I was off the path and on a snow field. Fuck. I was off and running, get out of there.

I was down bent low in the snow. Heard another crack and fuck me I could swear I felt a whizz. But he lost more time. I was terrified only I was ahead.

Went running straight on ahead. Bad plan. It was open field. Snow underneath was a foot deep. Got to go forward though never go back, hoped the snowing kept me hidden. Across that field, away from the railway heading wherever. Running and weaving and ducking. One moment I turned for looking and there the fucker was, skiing on down behind. He was coming.

I ran till I nearly croaked it in that snow. Then trees came up. Fence was broken down under the snow. I was in there. Running still.

Then I stopped. Till now I never got time for thinking. Wished I still never had. Gasping held my breath. Heart pounding racing away. Brain round in circles. Body knackered running through that snow. I was shitless again. Try and hold it together. Deal with the fucker or I was gone. Keep quiet and think.

He never could clock me in the dark trees when he was in the field. I picked up a branch, big fucker, waited for making my play. Heard him coming behind skiing into the trees. Slowly now. Still on his skis in the wood making his way hesitant. Heard him very close. Clocked the end of his skis. Three feet away.

I stepped out. I whacked him with my branch across his hooter. Hard as you like. Hard as I could.

He screamed out. Bernard. Where I butted him before now I whacked him full force. Then I was away. No point waiting for seeing if he dropped his rifle. I ran on further. Deeper in the trees. Dropping down now.

Dropping down?

All of a sudden I clocked where we were headed.

Wondered Bernard could clock anything through his blood. Wondered he understood what was happening here.

He was still skiing. Slowly slowly through the trees he made his slushing noises, making his way fumbling stumbling. Watched him. Kept his rifle in his right mitt, looking round best he could with his torch on top.

I was flat down behind a tree under a bush. Never find me there all night in the dark. No noise. Stopped my gasping. Heart thumping only kept my breath down. Silent watching him.

He skied on past. First slowly then he was gaining speed again. Faster. And I knew why. He never stopped himself on account of he never realized. Speeded up down that slope reckoned on catching up maybe.

Faster.

Then he was gone.

He was gone for good.

Thousand feet gone. Two thousand three thousand feet gone, who gives a fuck how many feet gone. He was gone. He skied off in space. Like a bird except he never flapped his wings. Biggest ski jump in history, the flying skier. He found they still got their precipices one each side the valley, one from Murren one from near Wengen. Very very big precipices indeed.

What goes up got to go down.

He went down.

18

Paulette was waiting for me by the train station in Wengen.

I walked back down.

'Nicky,' she goes.

Noreen stood beside her. Came over and took my hand in her glove. Nearly made me fucking blub.

'You best come indoors,' she went.

'Nicky that Rupert came back down,' Paulette turned round and said. 'I saw him go down the road.'

'Bernard ain't coming,' I goes.

'Nicky — ' went Noreen.

'I never touched him.' Been rehearsing my story on the way down. 'He never took account of the dangers of the mountains.'

She was looking very doubtful only just the one time now she was keeping it down. Even she cuddled me up. And it not being Christmas.

Then I clocked something very nasty indeed. Reminded me our troubles were never over yet. Over by the station were some fascists.

Same Mile End intellectuals made a go for

me and Jimmy Foley in The Coffee House up
Selborne Walk. Four of them. And they
clocked us clocking them.

★   ★   ★

So we got a lot of enemies here. Fuck alone
knew how they got here, they together or not
or just out for a fucking stroll. Never
mattered. What mattered was they were after
sorting us. Sorting me. Sorting it so it never
needed sorting again.

There was:
Rupert.
Mickey Cousins.
Tweedledum and fucking Tweedledum-
mer.
Four security.
Three boxers.
Four fascists.

15

On our side:
Paulette.
Rameez.
Afzal and Aftab.
TT.
Me.

Noreen?

7

No fucking contest. We kill 'em.
Then Jimmy Foley walked up.
'Jesus Nicky,' he goes. 'You never feel the cold or what in them clothes? Ain't this some fuckin' spot? I clocked them geezers up Selborne Walk again looking out for you mate. Same ones as before come after us, must've got bail. I followed them I'm telling you. Followed them all the way up Dover. Good job I got little Wayne Sapsford with me, borrowed us a fuckin' smart BMW for following them. Got a full tank in the bargain. They got an Audi. We got on a fuckin' boat in Dover. Followed them up Calais. Followed them across all them countries. Followed them up here. Left the motor down the bottom there, they don't let no motors up here you know that? Got on a fuckin' train. Came up here and that train brought us straight to you mate, worked out sweet innit?'
He finished.
'Yo Jimmy,' I goes. 'Reckon you got here just in time mate. And you Wayne innit.' Wayne came off the square. He was kind of fidgety, got the twitches on account of there were never any motors up Wengen. Wayne

never liked being anywhere he never got motors.

We all went up our hotel and ordered coffee off room service. We already arranged for meeting TT.

★   ★   ★

It looked like crisis time. And we reckoned we got to be ready before they were ready. Rule number one. Get your fucking retaliation in first.

We planned up our suite. TT brought George Marshall in with him. Made ten of us.

'Jesus George,' I went.

'This is most irregular,' he went. 'I must be bleeding mad coming out here when TT called me. I must be soft in the head. And too old by half. All for a bloody little rascal like you Nicky.'

'Leave it out George,' I goes. 'Try not getting too emotional about it geezer. Know how you feel but we're all fellers together here, don't want no tears and that.'

'Give me some of that coffee please Noreen,' he goes.

Good job we got plenty of space in that suite after all. I got more coffee. I was knackered and I was shocked. Shocked on account of the support. Still I wished I never came up Wengen in my life. Wished I was spending New Year's Eve down the fucking Palmerston same as usual. Wished I could take Noreen home after for a spot of shagging and a good sleep. Never wanted to be spending the evening fighting big geezers in the middle of the fucking mountains.

Still there we were. And seeing as there we were, it was best we shafted them.

'Look,' TT turned round and said. 'There are a lot of people chasing you Nicky it seems. We must protect you. This is partly my fault. We've got to get the police in. The Swiss police.' Same as usual no one took notice of TT. I never heard anything so fucking leery.

'Nicky,' goes Rameez. 'We got to get tooled up.'

'Tooled up,' goes Afzal.

'Huh,' goes Aftab.

'Oh my God,' goes TT.

'Then we got to plan the place of combat,' Rameez carries on. 'They take you inside here, they big strong geezers, you gone.'

'You the expert Rameez.'

'You got to be outside. Not likely they all carrying. Even so we stop them shooting. We got to hit them hard and early. What we got?'

We looked round. What we got? Paulette brought out an ice axe. 'Jesus,' went TT.

It looked like the business end of an ice axe was something you could do business with.

Jimmy nicked a couple of ski poles off the train station. Up Switzerland you always left your gear anyhow on account of nobody nicked anything.

Aftab shifted. Then he picked up something he laid behind the settee. It was a crossbow. Fucking great thing he borrowed out the tourist office. Hardly lift it. Kill you at two hundred paces. Hoped it worked at two.

Then I laid out my souvenirs on the floor, got a dozen of them should be something for everyone.

Swiss army knives. Fifty-seven fucking varieties of blade on those knives. Open a fucking bottle top, cut your hair, stir your fondue and take your stones out of horses' hooves. Got to be something there you could use for gouging a geezer.

Everyone picked one up. Except Noreen.

'That Swiss shafter you borrowed me,' I goes to Rameez. 'Most unfortunate only it not available at present. You got any other metal yourself?'

'Why course Nicky,' he turned round and said. 'Why course I got one or two other little items.'

'Reckoned you might.'

'But don't mean I don't want my historic

souvenir back Nicky.'

Oh fuck. I nicked Rameez's motor one time by accident, be chasing me past the grave for it. Same now with his sticker it looked like.

Then the doorbell rang.

No one stood behind it to open it. Not favourite getting shot up. Then we sent TT to do the negotiations.

He stood to one side out of the line and he called out. 'Open up police!' he went.

'Now hang on here TT,' went George. 'You got to open it mate. You're inside this time, remember? People out there, they say, 'Open up police!' If they're police that is. You're inside so you ask who it is, right?'

'Sorry,' goes TT, caught up in the excitement. He started again. 'Who is it?' he goes.

'It's me,' goes Diana. 'I have come out of hospital and I want to help. Nicky is that you? Your voice has changed.'

TT looked through the spy hole then opened up.

Standing beside Diana was Andy my probation.

'I met this gentleman in the lift,' she turned round and said. 'He informed me that he had been responsible for you in the past Nicky. I have told him that he has done a fine job in turning you into a gentleman of strength and moral vigour. I believe he is here to help you too.'

About as much use in a ruck Andy as Mrs Shillingford. Come to think of it I'd back Mrs Shillingford any morning. Maybe he could give the fuckers some counselling, speak them to death.

'Staying out of trouble again Nicky I see,' he went. 'Nice to know my time hasn't been wasted. I heard there might be a problem here so I thought I could speak to the British consul when you need bail, that kind of thing. I only stop short of being a character witness.'

'Jesus Andy,' I went. 'Good of you mate. Matter of fact you got here just in time.'

Diana walked over a bit unsteady, mince pies a bit glazed. They upped her dose of happy pills.

'Diana,' goes Noreen. 'You come and sit by me. We got a bit of a problem here, got to get it sorted.'

'It is all my fault,' she goes.

'No it's all my fault,' goes TT.

'Anyone else?' I went. 'Anyone else's fault? Nah. Fuck it. Done now.'

'Where are my relatives?' Diana asked. 'Where are those loathsome Bernard and Rupert and Caravella? What plot are they hatching now?'

'Two of them hatched,' I goes. 'They out of the frame. Rupert though he on the loose.'

Noreen clocked me suspicious again, no doubt thinking I went round killing geezers.

Then we had a pause. We all sipped our coffees one moment sitting round. We all gave it reflections about our lives. Heavy duty. Took about twenty seconds.

Then Rameez goes: 'It is time!'

'Yeah!'

'See the time eleven-forty-five? We get out there!'

'Yeah!'

'They more than us but we stronger innit?' he goes. I was never too sure of that one, I reckoned all the fuckers were stronger than me. 'They crippled. They bust up. They . . . ' — he gave it thinking, came up with the trump — 'they in the wrong . . . '

Rameez never was in the right before. Reckoned it got to be one major plus sign.

'Where are we going?' Diana asked.

'Out on the street lady. Midnight celebrations and that. Sing a couple of songs. Fireworks.'

'Oh good. That will perk me up a lot, I do like some music. We used to sing round the piano at home in the old days you know. Christmas carols, old folk songs, it was lovely.'

'Be just like that I reckon. We get out there on the square then eh?'

We all went downstairs in a troop. Wilhelm and Heidi were back behind the desk again tonight. 'Ah Nicky how good that I am seeing you again!' cries little Heidi.

Noreen looking round like a piranha fish. Heidi never noticed. Body like fresh plums.

We went out on the street. It made up a bit of a square where their High Street was wider. We stood there on one side, dozen of us waiting for the celebrations. Me and Noreen and Diana and Rameez and Afzal and Aftab and Andy and TT and George and Paulette and Jimmy and Wayne.

'You sure about this Noreen?' I went.

'Stand by your man,' she goes. 'Ain't no crime standing by your man.'

Old-fashioned bird Noreen after all.

The festivities already started. From one side came a procession. Traditional local people celebrating New Year. Collection of the most mournful-looking birds and geezers you ever clocked. All in that costume. All carrying great heavy cow bells round their necks. All singing, slow and gloomy. They trudged round the street and in a couple of restaurants winding round ringing their bells. Custom it seemed like. Get in there and invite everyone for some miserable dancing.

All the people goggled. They came back out. Tourists and Swiss all round the square.

Then they cleared off in another eater. And what did we clock on the far side?

All together. Strung out in a line.

Thirteen heavies. Four security and three boxers and four fascists and Tweedledum and Tweedledummer. Then Mickey Cousins and Rupert. Bandage on his arm.

And they got a few other bandages. Three boxers limping bad. Tweedledum and Tweedledummer keeping their bonces very still. Fascists never knew what they were doing anyhow. Only security looking big. And security never that big natural, only came with steroids.

Still bigger than me. And harder.

'Rameez you take them security,' I goes.

'No problem Nicky.'

They started coming over the square, then a voice came from behind me.

'Nicky my brother!' it went. 'Now that I am finding you here at last man! And now it is you is looking like you need some of my elementary guidance on life! You not tangling with they tiefing capitalist bastards again I is hoping!'

'Slip . . . Jesus Slip. The fuck you spring from? You released?'

'I is released just three days after Christmas

275

man, getting back that little sweet police custody time and all that good behaviour bollocks time course! Now I is hearing off your little sister what I went round to see, now I is hearing where you was, and I telling you man for a white girl your sister quite a classy little number innit?'

'Slip you never want to mess with her while that Rameez over there on her trail. He a psycho.'

'No problem! He my brother too! Now what we got here anyhow Nicky, some little social disturbance or what I am thinking?'

'Slip, you on licence after that release? You not supposed to be in any difficulty?'

'So I is hearing. Not supposed to be over them seas either I is hearing!' He giggled very amused. 'I report back next week my probation, she all right.'

'Report here to probation you want. Over there see.'

'Nicky you ain't half getting cool relations with your probation man. You take him on holidays and he fight in your social disturbances? Very cool indeed brother.'

'They coming Slip.'

'Right ahead bro'. Let them be right ahead.'

They came. Two hundred fucking witnesses round that square clocked them coming to us meaning business. We were innocent anyone could testify. Tourists started getting out the way now, no one wanting a chat with some limping boxer. They all clocked them though, the aggressors.

Mickey Cousins and Rupert still together. How the fuck they knew each other? They were coming for me and Diana. Rupert no problem except for maybe Rameez's souvenir he was holding. Mickey got a metal bar and Tweedledum and Tweedledummer. They came and they swung. I caught Mickey's bar half on my mitt. Hurt. I grabbed his wrist. Then I plunged up his arm with the Swiss army knife, straight in. Sudden blood spurted. Christ I struck a fucking artery. Got lucky right at the start.

He howled, swung at me, blood everywhere. Got me on the neck. I went down numb.

Noreen came towards me trying to get between. Then one instant I clocked a vision. Mickey Cousins coming down on me snarling then sudden Mickey Cousins disappearing off, tossed away in his own blood like some old ski.

It was Trudi. 'Ha ha Nicholas!' she goes chortling, same as usual. 'You are still in a pickle then isn't it? I can see I am having to sort you out again my boy. I only came up here for the New Year's Eve and what am I finding? Oh dear oh dear Nicholas. Oh dear oh dear.' She cackled again, great entertainment.

'Nicky who is this blonde?' hisses Noreen. 'Fit bleeding goddess you tell me who it is quick then eh?'

'That my bleeding ski instructor innit? Got a kid two months old.' My neck all numb.

'Huh.'

While Noreen was still yacking to me Trudi was guarding so I could get up slow. Boxer came towards us still limping, fists up and got a blackjack in one. Traditional geezer, I never clocked fists or a blackjack in years. Trudi got him with one of her aerobics, not so traditional, high kick up the chin sent him back down a while.

Rameez and Afzal and Aftab in a proper mixer with security. Everything you used on nightclubs security got, blades and rice flails and baseball bats, the monte. Only they moved slow and they were never as vicious. It got rough in there. I sent TT over for the numbers. We needed more.

George did his boxing at school forty years before, trying his form now, sizing up his short-arm jabs on another boxer. Never the way for best results. Wayne Sapsford came round behind the fucker, hit him with a postcard stand he borrowed outside a shop. No postcards in it. Fucker went down and Wayne put the boot in.

Fascists were no fucking danger anyhow. Same as always, you stood up to them and they got no fucking attitude. Before they even made their move Paulette and Jimmy went at them, same as in Selborne Walk. Paulette buried her ice axe in a geezer's shoulder. While he howled out Jimmy put his ski pole straight in the fucker's mince pie. One less.

I was stood with Noreen one side Trudi the other. Mickey Cousins no problem for a minute. I clocked one security lying down very still over there so now we outnumbered them, no contest.

Three fascists were coming our way though. One of them got a blade on me, nasty automatic number. I stopped him got my arm cut. Paulette whacked him from behind with her axe, just pulled it out the other geezer, this time hit the fucker with the flat bit. Straight on the skull, thank you and goodnight.

Slip came up on another. He never wasted his time when he was in nick. Fit as a fucking banshee. Fucker went down in a rain of blows and kicks and little stabbings. Then all of a sudden came a crack. And a big silence over the whole square.

Rupert's rifle.

He was never so safe after all.

Except with only one good arm he never aimed straight. He aimed for Diana. Jimmy just then running across making for a boxer who got on top of George trying to bite him. Minding his own business. Rupert shot him in the back.

It was one thing shooting your own kind. Another thing shooting geezers from Walthamstow. It was very very serious aggravation indeed.

Maybe fifteen seconds later Rupert lay there in red snow. We all left what we were doing before. He never got time for bringing his rifle up again. We were all wearing boots and carrying. Least we carried was Swiss army knives and they got a lot of implements on them. Most of their implements got used on Rupert, we maybe even got a stone out of his hoof. Fifteen seconds.

Rupert might be alive, he might be brown bread.

Either way, two hundred fucking witnesses clocked it was self-defence.

Then Noreen, not involved in all that, turned round and said, 'Give me that army knife Nicky.'

I did.

She pulled out the scissors. Then she went over to Rupert laying there on his side.

She cut his dick off.

She pulled down his trousers and his underpants in the snow. Then she opened out those scissors. She knelt down and she closed those scissors again round it and she squeezed and she squeezed. No joy. So she stood up and she put them in place again, sideways up. It was one of their big knives, big scissors. So she got them in place and then she got his leg underneath for a table. Then she raised up her little foot and she stamped down so hard on the handle of those scissors you wanted to cry out loud.

Then she looked down and then she left, satisfied with her work. It was done.

She came back and she stood beside me.

'Noreen,' I went, shaking slightly.

'Yes Nicky?'

'Er, you mind telling me why you just did that?'

'No problem Nicky. You want your knife back?'

'No . . . maybe not bother Noreen. Get my mum another one.' I waited for her explaining.

'First,' she goes. She was quiet, composed like.

'Yeah?'

'He killed his brother. No business doing that, family values.'

'Yeah.'

'Next he tried to kill Diana. My friend innit?'

'Yeah.'

'Then he went after my man. Not allowed.'

Still a bit harsh I reckoned. Geezer to geezer it was, not so drastic.

'And I reckoned he never do any of that if he was missing a bit. You reckon geezers ever fight when they never got that part attached? Biggest part of the problem Nicky.'

Jesus H.

I was still wondering Rupert was alive or brown bread. Plenty blood and he was quiet. And working on him being alive, could they put it back? Heard they did wonders these days.

After that we were never likely losing the ruck. Their side never got the spirit any more, no chance winning when your leader never got a dick. We went in whacking. Rameez so happy he was singing. Got his souvenir back off Rupert now and he was slicing wild.

Mickey Cousins was over the other side slipping away staggering trailing blood. Headed for the High Street.

'Aftab!' I goes.

Aftab never got a proper opportunity for his crossbow till now. He never got a fucking clue how it worked, still he wound it up and loaded it and he ran part the way over and he pointed. Twenty yards off Mickey Cousins.

Fuck knows where he aimed or maybe he never aimed. It got Mickey right up the arse. Right up the crack. Must have been Aftab never wound it up full or it split him in two. As it goes it came out a very very sharp attack of piles.

Mickey cried out like nothing I ever heard.

*　*　*

It was all done now.

A couple ran off got away, the rest of their side lay there serious hurting. I hoped they got their holiday insurance.

Our side we were never damaged too bad it looked like. Afzal got a nasty stomach cut and my arm needed a bit of mending but only regulation.

Then I clocked one body in the snow I recognized. Old Bill.

TT moaning hard. Looked like a horse kicked his face. Maybe he tangled with some boxers. In the bargain he got one arm hanging off. Only one weapon there likely for doing that. Rameez's souvenir when it was borrowed by Rupert.

Justice all round it seemed like. Never too bad a wounded copper.

I went over to Jimmy Foley still lying there face down. 'Jimmy,' I goes.

'Nicky,' he turned round and said. 'This the fuckin' truth I got shot for you a second time? I got shot?'

'You got shot Jimmy. From where I'm standing I reckon it maybe not fatal.'

'That the case? You sure about that?'

'You still alive Jimmy. And it look like it only went in the side. How you so fuckin' lucky Jimmy when you get shot?'

'Ain't so fuckin' lucky from where I sees it Nicky. Ain't so fuckin' lucky getting shot at all.'

'You in pain Jimmy?'

'The fuck you think Nicky? Maybe not fuckin' fatal, still fuckin' painful.'

'Nah you just biased. Here, hotel staff coming over with their first aid, Red Cross and that. Have you right as rain.'

Then it struck twelve.

'Happy New Year Jimmy,' I goes. 'You make a wish?'

'Fuckin' fuck off Nicky,' he goes. 'All I wish.'

∗　∗　∗

Then the Swiss Old Bill arrived. Two of them very smart. Not the same geezers as up the

284

hotel before so they got at least four. Then the doctors and nurses.

Nobody moved far. We were in for a long spell. Only Slip got missing quiet, went off on account of he was on that licence. Rest of us got nothing to hide. Except a few weapons we disposed of temporary. Innocent party it got to be no problem.

Geezer came round with his hot toddies. Happy hour came late that night.

Diana sitting down in the snow regardless. Happy at last. Everyone else round the outside waiting.

Noreen came over leaned beside me squeezed my arm. Bit unfortunate made all the blood ooze out. 'Reckon you sorted them problems after all,' she went.

Blood and sweat dripping off me all together. Never felt like I sorted any problems. I was fucking stuffed.

Glad I got my bird there though. 'Noreen . . . ' I went.

'Yeah?'

'You want one of them hot toddies doll?'

'Don't mind.'

'Then a spot of yodelling?'

'Yeah. Now you mention it Nicky. Spot of yodelling suit me right well.'

Maybe in the morning take in some more of that skiing.

IT WAS AN ACCIDENT

Jeremy Cameron

After four years of incarceration, Nicky Burkett is released onto the sunny streets of North London's most edgy area: Walthamstow. The guy wants to go straight. The beautiful Noreen Hurlock wants him to go straight — in fact, she vows she won't come near him if he doesn't. So he tries. But events and people conspire against him. The 'work' he is offered proves dodgy. He is attacked. His mates are attacked. Even running to Jamaica isn't enough to keep him out of trouble. The time has come for the fight back to begin . . .

VINNIE GOT BLOWN AWAY

Jeremy Cameron

A Walthamstow native, nineteen-year-old Nicky Burkett has been in and out of trouble his whole life. When he finds the body of his best mate, Vinnie, at the bottom of a tower block minus his feet, Nicky's code of conduct dictates that he exact an appropriate revenge. The problem is, he's seriously outgunned — it would seem that Vinnie crossed some deadly criminals who have decided to take over the drug trade in the area. So Nicky sets out to persuade his allies and acquaintances to join his vendetta. But things don't go according to plan . . .